The Jefferson Letters

The Jefferson Letters

༄༅

by

John Ballinger

THE JEFFERSON LETTERS. Copyright © 2001 by John Ballinger.
All rights reserved. Printed in the United States of America.
No part of this book may be used or reproduced in any manner whatsoever
without written permission from the publisher.

Library of Congress Catalog Card Number: 2001086096

ISBN # 0-87517-114-1

Printed by The Dietz Press
Richmond, Virginia

First Edition

For Lisa Ann Pershing Ballinger,
a source of great joy.

The Jefferson Letters

Prologue

*H*e had travelled through France and Italy and along most of the American Eastern seaboard, but he'd never seen as lovely a place as Williamsburg, Virginia, at four o'clock in the morning: the fog rising from the cobblestones on Nicholson Street; the enveloping quiet of a town asleep; the peaceful solitude of eighteenth century buildings seen by dim street lamps; everything ordered: white picket fences separating private gardens, the entire town arranged in pleasing and human proportions, both with its individual buildings and as a whole, each structure relating to the others as if they were family, which in a profound way, they are: separate entities, complete in themselves, but dependent on each other for a greater life and destiny.

He stood motionless staring at a light-grey horned owl, who was sitting in a lower branch of an old, gnarled oak tree, his head turning in great arcs, his eyes unblinking, searching the lamp-lit street for the nocturnal scurrying of a mouse or other small rodent, a living body to sacrifice his life to the owl, giving him sustenance, keeping him alive for one more day.

In the past few years, he had spent a considerable amount of time silently observing nature like this. He found it ironic because for most of his life he was the one who was being watched—besieged really—surrounded by friends and foes, all of whom courted him and his vanity, waiting for an opportunity to ask for something in return. Early on, he had learned to accept the game. It is, after all, *the nature of politics, and he was a political animal. But even at its worst, when the appeal of these sycophants was at its strongest, he fought against being totally enveloped by people. He carved out time for himself to read, to write letters to his friends, to study, and to reflect. Time alone with his own thoughts was sacred, and he has never tired of such solitude, even though he now had hours in abundance for his private meditations.*

This is not to imply he was ever a reclusive man. He enjoyed sharing good talk, good food, and good wine with friends, possibly at times more than he should. But always there were the quiet hours for contemplation, like now, silently watching an owl in the middle of Williamsburg at four o'clock in the morning.

Normally, he would have waited to see the owl inevitably swoop down from his branch to claw and devour its prey, but he was upset and preoccupied. He had seen something distressing the morning before, and he had been walking around the town ever since, thinking of what he could do about it.

So he left the owl alone to its own devices, and walked along Nicholson Street until he reached the Public Gaol. Then he took the foot bridge toward the Capitol and from there walked the length of the Duke of Gloucester Street until he came to the Wren Building. He passed the Printery, Chowning's Tavern, the Courthouse, and Bruton Parish Church, buildings more than etched in his memory, buildings now, after so many years, a part of him.

On the way back, in Merchant's Square, he stopped at the sign of Parker's Rare Books. A ginger-colored cat sat in the window looking out on the Duke of Gloucester Street. Its eyes seemed to follow him as he walked past. He stopped. He wasn't certain, so he went back to the window. He stuck out his hand to the glass, with his index finger extended. The cat came over and sniffed at the window where he was pointing. The cat saw him and seemed to sense his mood.

Then, the man smiled for the first time since he had seen those accursed letters. He knew, as much as anyone can know such things, he was going to come back to this bookshop and he would receive help here. He found it ironic he was about to go and see a bookseller for help with his problem. He had despised the trade when he was younger. He found booksellers cunning and greedy in their dealings with customers. He thought their knowledge shallow. In his experience, book dealers drew very little from the books they sold, content to know the author's name, the title, and most importantly, the price for which they could sell the book. He had never met a bookseller who pondered or thought deeply about philosophy or science. As scholars, booksellers were as country carpenters to great architects. And now he was about to ask one of them to help save his reputation. God and the Universe surely knew the meaning of the word "irony."

He moved past Parker's front door to the windows on the other side. The windows faced a walkway between the bookshop and the adjoining restaurant. The cat's gaze followed him, calmly, expectantly. Then the man stopped. He had to prepare himself. He had to think about how he was going to approach this Parker. His cat accepted him, but would he? The man wondered what he would do if the situation were reversed? It gave him pause.

"Parker's Rare Books," the sign read. "Antiquarian Booksellers— Brad Parker, Proprietor." The man turned to walk away. He was still uncertain. Surely, he was no longer a part of the world of his youth, where reputation mattered, where "personal integrity" and "honor" were real concepts necessary for advancement. He was no longer a part of this life, yet he surprised himself with how much his reputation still mattered to him. He knew then he could not just walk away and allow someone to unfairly besmirch it. But coming back to this bookshop and exposing his situation? It was equally egregious.

He walked back down the Duke of Gloucester Street toward the Capitol. The sun had not yet risen. Still, it was turning the sky into ever lightening shades of grey. The man had much to think about and much to decide, but the ginger-colored cat in the bookshop window had given him hope.

Chapter One

The letter was neatly written on one large sheet of paper and ended with the bold signature of Thomas Jefferson.

"It's nice," I said flatly. It was, of course, more than nice. It was magnificent. The letter was dated 22 January 1804, and it was written to John Adams. Jefferson apparently had given Adams previous, detailed instructions for negotiating an important matter with an unnamed third party. The letter stressed the importance of Adams carrying out Jefferson's earlier instructions in every detail. "I wish I could be with you in this matter, but I cannot," Jefferson wrote. "Therefore, I place my entire trust in you, and you alone. My thoughts and profound hopes rest on your shoulders." Then Jefferson signed his name. It sounded important. I had no idea what the negotiations were, but I was reasonably sure, with a little research, I could find out.

"I want to sell the letter," Abbe Mosley said. She sat in one of two straight-backed chairs opposite my desk. Mrs. Mosley wore a white, frilly blouse under a red blazer on which the insignia of Ferguson Real Estate was boldly embroidered on a pocket over her heart. The outfit was a corporate look, designed, I'm sure, to make the sales agent look both pert and efficient. I thought its color clashed miserably with Abbe Mosley's natural skin tone, and her nervous drumming on the chair made her look anything but professional.

To be fair, her nervousness was probably due to the confusion I was projecting. "But what about Peter?" I asked. Peter Mosley was her husband. He, like me, was also a dealer in rare books and manuscripts.

"This is mine," Abbe snapped.

"I'm sure it is, but why not let Peter sell it for you?"

"Because if I did, I'd never see a penny from the sale," Abbe shot back.

Knowing Peter Mosley, I had no doubt she was right. I had yet to meet a bookseller who admitted he liked or trusted him. The mention of Peter Mosley's name at a book fair was usually good for another "terrible-Peter" story. Over the years I had heard dozens. I can't recall one bookdealer ever saying a kind word about the man, which means a lot in a profession of diverse people who, politically, range from left of Ted Kennedy, to right of David Duke.

Peter Mosley came off as snide, arrogant, and smarmy. I habitually counted the books on my shelves after he visited the shop. Abbe's remark didn't surprise me. The fact she was still married to him *did*. I remembered their wedding seven years ago. Abbe was only twenty-three then. Sometimes it takes time to admit a mistake to yourself, I reasoned, especially when you're young and still believe you can change the man you love.

"This transaction will be between you and me," Abbe Mosley said. "It's none of Peter's business."

I nodded.

"I want fifty-five hundred dollars for the letter," she quickly added. "I have a separate money-market account in my name. You can wire payment directly to it."

"Not a problem," I replied, hopefully not too quickly. Part of my bookseller's brain had been trying to conjure up a price to offer for the letter. I was thinking about some kind of consignment arrangement, wondering how large of a seller's fee I could ask. Obviously, Abbe Mosley had already given the matter some thought and had opted for instant money rather than holding out for top dollar. This was fine with me. Buying a Jefferson letter is like buying cash. It's incredibly easy to sell.

There was still the matter of its authenticity. The letter looked real to me, but so did Dolly Parton's breasts. I had been in business long enough to realize I was not a manuscript expert, and this letter had been in Peter Mosley's house. The proximity worried me.

"Abbe," I said. "I will buy the letter for fifty-five hundred dollars, but my offer's conditional." Her face sagged. "I need to send it to a manuscript appraiser to verify it's genuine."

"Of course it's genuine."

"Then there's no problem."

"How long will it take before you'll know?" I heard overtones of panic in Abbe's voice.

"Two days," I replied calmly. "I'll send it Overnight UPS. I should hear something no later than tomorrow evening. You'll have the money in your bank account by Wednesday."

"Two days, then." Abbe Mosley got out of her chair and offered me her hand with all the pertness her red jacket had promised.

"And I'd like you to sign this," I said, reaching into my desk for a copy of a purchase agreement. I hardly ever used one, but the thought of Peter lurking in the background made me wary. "It's just a formality." I filled in the blanks and handed it to her.

Abbe sat again and read it carefully. Real estate agents paid attention to legal paperwork.

"All it says is if the letter's real, I'll buy it for fifty-five hundred dollars; I have the letter in my possession; and the letter is legally yours to sell."

Abbe took the pen I had given her and signed in the appropriate spot. Her signature wasn't as bold or self-assured as Jefferson's, but it was fine by me.

G. Gordon Kitty, the bookshop cat, walked into my office. From the corner of my eye I could see Gordon pick up his head, sniff at

Abbe Mosley, and walk back out. Gordon had an instinct for when he could expect a good petting. He had obviously decided this was not one of those moments.

"Thank you for coming to me with the letter," I said.

"There may be more," Abbe replied.

Her remark was vague and cryptic. It took a second for it to register. "More Jefferson letters?" I asked.

"There's a stack of them," she said, holding her fingers four and a half inches apart.

"Good God, Abbe! Where did you find them?" I shouldn't have reacted so strongly, but even though Jefferson spent hours each day writing to his many friends and acquaintances, good letters by him were not common, everyday finds, and large bundles like the one Abbe described were unheard of.

All at once she became guarded. "I can't tell you where I got them, but I can assure you, the letters *are* rightfully mine." She stood, too anxious to sit, and I stood with her.

"I'm sorry this is so uncomfortable for you," I said.

"I'm going to divorce Peter," Abbe blurted out. She said it with a mixture of determination and angst. Her tone was disconcerting. "I'm trying to build a little cash reserve before I tell him."

"Peter doesn't know?"

"He might know I'm unhappy, but he wouldn't guess 'divorce.' Self-centered fools rarely do."

"I think you're underestimating Peter," I said with little conviction. The truth was, Abbe was most likely right on target.

"But once I tell him, his mood will change. Peter is competitive. He hates to lose—lose anything. You know, Brad, sometimes I feel he thinks I'm just one of his rare books. Living with Peter, I know what it must have been like to be a slave." Then a flash of panic, which seemed to live just below Abbe's surface, erupted again. "Brad, don't tell him about my plans!"

"I wouldn't, Abbe," I reassured her.

"I don't want him to suspect anything until I'm ready."

"Are you afraid of him?" I asked.

Abbe seemed focused within herself. "Peter's unpredictable," she said. "I have to get everything in order before I spring it on him."

"Are you afraid he'd physically harm you?"

Abbe didn't reply, but her silence said more than words. "There are organizations, Abbe, homes for battered women."

"They wouldn't stop Peter."

"But—"

"It's nice of you to worry, Brad," Abbe said, attempting a smile. "But I really do have a plan and I think everything will be fine."

We left it there. I walked Abbe downstairs.

"Two days?" she asked at the door.

"Earlier, if I can get confirmation by telephone."

"Good!"

The shop was empty. I walked back to the packing area where Bruce was absent-mindedly scratching Gordon behind his ears. Bruce was my office manager. Gordon had found a willing hand, after all. "I just might have bought us a Jefferson letter," I said.

"How do you 'just might have bought' something?" he asked.

"Needs to be appraised first."

"If it's Mosley's letter, it's probably a good idea."

"Et tu, Bruce," I thought.

From my office, I called Keith Stanley. With shops in New York, Los Angeles, and Las Vegas, he sold more autographs and manuscripts than any other dealer in the country. I had known him for twenty years. His secretary gave me his telephone number *du jour*. I reached him on the second ring and he agreed to give me an "instant take," as he put it, on Jefferson's letter as soon as it arrived. It was two-thirty.

On my way out, I handed Bruce the letter along with Stanley's address.

"Send it UPS Overnight."
"Lunch?" Bruce asked.
"Chez Bayou."

Chapter Two

❦

Chez Bayou Restaurant is on Jamestown Road, a mile and a half from Merchant's Square. Its architecture is Old-Rural-Southern. The front of the building has a covered porch, which extends along its entire length. Inside it has broad-planked flooring held together by wooden pegs and in all three dining-rooms, rustic wainscotting. You'd think Chez Bayou's building was a hundred and fifty years old, but it was actually constructed to be a restaurant in the nineteen-sixties.

It was mid-October and Chez Bayou had been open for fourteen months. It took Kate Whitney and her two partners four additional months to prepare for the opening. Being in Williamsburg was an experiment for Kate. It was risky business on many levels—a new restaurant, new partners, a new region of the country, and a new relationship with me.

Kate and I had shared history. Thirty years earlier we had been neighbors. I had worked with her ex-husband, Charles, at the CIA. Kate and I became friends, partly to commiserate our both being in bad marriages, but back then we weren't ready to do anything about it. I had two young children. My lustful thoughts toward Kate never got beyond flirtation. Then, three years ago, we met again in Austin, Texas. Kate had divorced. Meeting in such an unexpected way seemed like fate. Kismet. The old smoldering feelings rekindled, and this time there was nothing to hold us back. But we left Texas separately. Kate went to Los Angeles; I, home to Williamsburg, Virginia. We frequently talked on the telephone and met for long weekends, once in Chicago and once in New York. Then Kate made a decision to open a new restaurant in Williamsburg.

I was ecstatic. It sounded like a great plan, and for the most part it was. The business, Chez Bayou, was a success from the beginning, but our relationship was in need of some work. It had been bouncing along like a sputtering car with a faulty fuel pump.

It was hard for me to understand what exactly was wrong between us. We would go for long periods, growing closer and more content. Then, just when everything seemed right, Kate would get annoyed and bombard me with a laundry list of criticisms, delivered with a venom far out of proportion with my supposed crime.

Once, when we were away for a weekend, I had gotten annoyed and yelled at a hotel clerk—not the act of a mature man, but not a mortal sin either. Kate was livid. I was fine five minutes after it had happened, but it took two weeks for Kate to begin talking to me again. Kate thawed slower than an iceberg in arctic waters.

Looking back, I counted four such crises during the past eighteen months and the yo-yo effect was bothersome. We went from being lovers to strangers and then back again. Still, I didn't want to leave.

I remembered when I was fourteen and our family vacationed on the Connecticut coast. I swam almost every day in a small horseshoe bay which fed into Long Island Sound. At the end of the summer, I and three of my friends challenged each other to swim across the bay's open end.

We all dove into the water together. I could hear my three friends beside me, but because I was the strongest swimmer, I eventually took the lead. I had been concentrating on making my strokes long and smooth until, half way across the bay, I had begun to tire. I looked around for my companions. I finally found them. They were climbing back on the rocks where we had started. I was alone in deep water, over my head.

I can still remember the grip of panic I felt. Back then I had been able to convert my fears into adrenalin and swim to the other side. It was a valuable lesson. The incident taught me not to panic and to focus on a problem with as much intensity as it took to get it solved.

The lesson worked at the CIA, where I advanced rapidly. It wasn't quite as effective for me in relationships. I felt the same childhood panic again during Kate's lengthy withdrawals. I realized if Kate and I stayed together, there were times I was going to feel alone and over my head in deep water, and it scared the hell out of me. I loved Kate, but lingering doubts were sending up red warning flags I couldn't ignore.

And then, in an instant, Kate would return to her old self, things would be better between us and I would forget my doubts until the next time.

Kate and I kept separate apartments. On most evenings, we would sleep together at one place or the other. Inevitably, something we wanted would be at the other location. It was a minor annoyance, but it wasn't enough for us to rush and move in together, which is another way of saying we weren't ready yet for a greater commitment. But we did try to meet for lunch whenever it was possible.

Kate wasn't at the restaurant when I arrived. The dining room was empty except for Kate's two partners, a large black man with the unlikely name of Napoleon Robespierre Jones, and his wiry companion, Chili Rodriguez.

They were as unlikely a trio as had ever started a restaurant together. Napoleon and Chili were ex-cons, and Kate was a lady. They all met in Paris, France, as students of *Escoffier Ecole*, a prestigious and overpriced French cooking school. Despite their different backgrounds, they shared similar values and attitudes toward work and food, and decided to create Chez Bayou together.

"You got to take it easy on the pot boys," Napoleon was saying to Chili when I arrived.

"Wha' you know?"

"The last one was the third in two weeks. He quit like the others."

"Well, find a fourth, then."

"Chili, it ain't easy to find the help. You throw knives at them, it becomes harder."

"He was whistling," Chili responded. "I told him to stop the noise. He didn't. So I threw a knife at him. So wha'?" The problem with being around Chili wasn't his twisted logic; the problem was the rest of us couldn't quite grasp his reasoning quick enough to avoid the inevitable consequences.

"Maybe he didn't stop whistling because he didn't think you were serious," Napoleon explained.

"So! He knows I was serious now!"

"Yep! You got the point across. And now he's gone. Now we got to find another pot boy and train him."

"Hey! Butt out! I ran a kitchen bigger than this one. I didn't have no problems there."

Napoleon sat back and laughed. It was an easy laugh rumbling up from his large belly. Napoleon wasn't fat. He was "large"—six foot five, two hundred and eighty pounds, with massive shoulders and legs. He told me once he had played football at Lafayette College. He was in his late thirties now, past his prime for football, but I could still envision him playing. He had the build. "Chili, you just so much bullshit!" he said. "You ran a kitchen in Sewell State Prison. Pot boys couldn't quit on you. They was mostly doing three to five."

"What's your point?" Chili asked.

"I get you one more pot boy," Napoleon said. "My point is—he quits, I don't get no more pot boys for you. *You* clean the pots yourself. Understand?"

"Shit!"

"Understand?" Napoleon repeated.

"Wonder what Miss Kate would say?"

"No Miss Kate. This is between you and me, brother." The warmth of Napoleon's laugh had vanished, and Chili had noticed. "Now, one more time," he said slowly and evenly. "You understand?"

There was a long silence. "Shit!" Chili said defiantly.

Napoleon pointed his index finger at him. "If pot boy number four goes, you the man scrubs the pots."

Chili turned to leave the room, "I unnerstand," he said over his shoulder as he got to the door.

When Napoleon saw me in the corner of the room, he smiled again. His laugh returned. "Brad, how long you been standing there?" he asked.

"Long enough," I said.

His laugh came naturally and unexpectedly like secondary shock waves from an earthquake. "My management lesson for the day," he said. "'The Ability to Persuade,' one of the eight characteristics of a successful person."

"You reading self-help books now?" I asked.

"Don't need to. I make my own self-help book as I go along."

I wondered what the other seven successful characteristics were, but I didn't ask.

I had known Napoleon for eighteen months and he was still an enigma to me. Both large and gentle, brash and caring, physical and intellectual, Napoleon Robespierre Jones was a mass of contradictions. He even intimated once he had been in Parker's Rare Books years before. When I pressed for details, he changed the subject and I had never been able to change it back. But if we were at war and I could choose my fox hole partner, it would be Napoleon. I know he would be there for me, no matter what.

I looked around the dining room. "Where's Kate?"

"Went for a doctor's appointment," Napoleon said. "She's late. What do you want for lunch?"

The food at Chez Bayou had added ten pounds to my weight during the past year. "Something light," I said.

"Got a vegetable platter. Chili baked some corn with butter and chili powder, red and orange peppers for color, onions, snow-peas, and God-knows what else, all dribbled with a marinade, and served over a bed of polenta. There's slaw on the side."

And it was why people put up with Chili. He touched food and turned it into magic. Napoleon turned the magic into words. They were quite a team.

Napoleon went to the kitchen and returned with the promised dish. The first bites were as good as advertised. Napoleon sat down. "Chili off for a walk. Cool himself down," Napoleon said.

"You met in prison, didn't you?" I asked. I knew part of the story from Kate, but Napoleon rarely talked to me about his life.

"Sewell State Prison. It's in Charleston."

Kate had told me the prison's name, but I don't even think she knew exactly why they were asked to be residents there. Napoleon wasn't about to volunteer any information on the whys either.

"Chili was in Sewell about a year before I got there, right after 'The Granton Incident.'"

I grunted to let Napoleon know I was listening, while I continued to eat.

"Before I came to Sewell, there was this tough prison guard, George Granton," Napoleon said. "Never met him, but he had a reputation for being one mean mother. And big! Bigger than me! Well, one day Chili came back to his cell. He was in charge of the kitchen back then. Had a lot of freedom. On his pillow, Chili found a Baby Ruth candy bar. Now, Chili was a con-wise inmate, so he didn't say nothing to nobody. He took the candy bar and hid it in a brick he had hollowed out next to his bunk. Then, he replaced the brick in the wall and waited.

"One day, a week later, Chili comes back to his cell after work and finds this Granton guy there sitting on his cot.

"'You got my present?' Granton asked.

"'Wha' present?' Chili asked back.

"'The candy bar.'

"'The candy bar,' Chili repeated. 'The Baby Ruth candy bar? You left it for me?'

"'Yeah.'

"'Thanks,' Chili said.

"'And I want it back,' Granton told him.

"By this time it's getting a little close in the cell. Chili's watching Granton. Granton's watching Chili—lustful like. Granton reached over and put his hand on Chili's thigh.

"'Hey!' Chili said, squeaking like he does. 'You want your Baby Ruth back, I buy you one.'

"'You don't understand,' Granton told him. 'I don't want just any old Baby Ruth. I want the one I gave you.'

"'Wha' if I don't have it?' Chili asked.

"'Then you just owe me a favor or two,' Granton said, reaching again for Chili's thigh.

"Chili slapped hard at Granton's hand. He understood the situation better now. Chili never had no fear, not since I knowed him, but Chili told me right then he was just plain scared. He turned around and took the hollowed out brick from the wall and grabbed the Baby Ruth bar from inside.

"'You want your Baby Ruth back, the one you gave me? Here!'

"Chili threw it in Granton's lap. Then he walked over and stood in front of Granton. He reached down and took the big man's balls in his hand and squeezed. Chili told me Granton tried to get up but Chili stood over him and shoved him back. Chili's small, but he knows how to use what he's got. He moved and pinned Granton's arms between his body and the bed. The big man supposed to have broken into a sweat with the pain and all. Finally, Chili got in

Granton's face and hissed. 'You ever try again, you'll disappear. Nobody even remember you were here. Now, get out!'

"There were two cons watching the last part, standing in the corridor outside the cell, their mouths wide open, their eyes buggin'. Granton was supposed to have stood up. He had his billy club in his hand. He was ready to do some damage, but then he saw the cons staring at him.

"'What are you looking at?' Granton said to them.

"The two cons froze. They couldn't talk. Then Granton got up and left. The story goes Chili reached down and picked up the Baby Ruth and threw it after Granton. 'You forgot this,' he told him. The candy bar hit Granton in the back and fell to the ground.

"Granton turned around. 'We ain't through with this yet, boy!' he told Chili."

"Then what happened?" I asked.

"Well, word got around the prison about Chili and Granton. Granton couldn't go any place without cons staring at him with their silent grins. The warden had the chaplain talk to Chili. He wanted to know unofficially what had happened. But Chili stayed true to the code. He didn't say nothing.

"Three days later, Chili was out on the loading platform looking at produce had just come in. Granton came out. He didn't have his arms pinned then. He had a billy club in his left hand and his service revolver in his right.

"Chili would have been seriously hurt or dead if three of the brothers hadn't been watching Granton stride through the kitchen. They knew something was going down, so they followed Granton out on the dock. Granton saw them before things got out of hand. He stood on the dock twenty feet or so from Chili and put his revolver back in its holster.

"'You're lucky again,' the brothers heard Granton say.

"'You ain't,' Chili told him in his high, nervous voice. 'I warned you. Tomorrow you disappear. Poof!'

"Was all anyone ever saw of George Granton."

"What do you mean?" I asked. "Granton vanished?"

"Gone!"

"Jesus! Where?"

"Well, it's the problem. Nobody knows. George Granton was one of those men who didn't pay much attention to paperwork or details. He never clocked out, never punched his time card. But I was told it wasn't unusual with Granton. Six guards testified they saw him leave Sewell at the end of his shift, even though his pickup truck was still in the prison parking lot the next morning. Two of his neighbors weren't sure, but they thought they remembered seeing him at a local gin-mill. But Granton didn't clock in for work the next morning, and like Chili predicted, nobody ever saw George Granton again."

"Do you know what happened?" I asked.

Napoleon shrugged his shoulders. "Hell, when I got to Sewell, there was a rumor Chili killed Granton, cut him into pieces and ground up the usable parts into meat loaf and sausage."

"Christ!"

"Was a good enough rumor nobody in Sewell State Prison ate anything resembling meat for two weeks, but nobody knew for sure. The warden talked to Chili. It was all official this time: tape recorders, lawyers, everything. But the warden never could prove nothin'. He couldn't bring charges. They weren't even sure Granton was in the prison. The whole matter was just kind of dropped."

"But didn't *you* ask Chili?"

"Nope! Guess I never felt it was none of my business." Napoleon hesitated. "Maybe, I just didn't want to know."

"Kate said you saved his life once, in prison."

Napoleon smiled. "A long story for another day. But I will say something—a man like Chili, he needs somebody to watch his back for him."

* * * * *

Kate came through the door at three-thirty. She didn't take four steps before I knew something was wrong. It was the way she moved. I couldn't put my finger on it—a subtle stiffness, a mechanical flow, a tiredness, as if she had spent the last few hours walking across the Sahara Desert. She attempted a smile.

"Hi," she said to me, walking over and giving me a kiss. It was a sisterly peck; there was no passion behind it. She looked down at my nearly empty plate. "What do you think of the curried corn?" she asked.

"You just had an opportunity to taste it yourself."

"Beggar." Kate reached down again and gave me a second kiss, this time with feeling. She ran her tongue over my lips. "Not bad," she said, but her smile quickly faded and she sat heavily on the chair to my right.

The lines at the corners of Napoleon's eyes deepened as he watched Kate. "What can I get you, babe?"

"I'm fine."

"Get you some tea," Napoleon continued. He stood, towering over us. As he walked around the table, he passed behind Kate's chair and casually caressed the back of her neck with his massive hand. "Tea always he'ps me."

Kate waited until Napoleon was through the kitchen's swinging door before she spoke. "Doctor Sallie took a long time with the physical," Kate said. Her face had lost most of its color. "She thinks she might have found a mass." Kate's eyes widened as she swallowed the last word.

"'Mass?' What do you mean 'mass?'" Kate's tenseness was contagious. Fear tingled through my body.

"She's not sure. I have an appointment for an ultra-sound tomorrow at the hospital."

"This 'mass'. Where is it?"

"It's near my ovaries. They'll know more tomorrow after the ultra-sound."

I wasn't certain what all this meant, but I knew by the look on Kate's face it was serious. "How big is this 'mass'?" I asked. I was making an attempt at being calm and analytical.

"She didn't say," Kate answered, "but it was large enough for her to find with her fingers."

"What's she afraid it might be?"

"Cancer." I noticed Kate's eyes were red. She had been crying. "Ovarian cancer."

We were both standing then. I put my arms around her. She began to sob. Her body shook from spasms, which passed through her to me.

* * * * *

Kate spent the night reading from *The Johns Hopkins Medical Handbook*. It was in the bookcase on her side of the bed. She consulted it regularly whenever either of us had any unusual medical symptoms. She was obsessively pro-active about her health. I wasn't. I made Kate angry. I didn't blame her. I wouldn't want to take care of someone who had become sick because he had refused to take a few preventative measures. So, I tried being better, but I was still light years away from Kate, probably a good indication as to why women live longer than men.

As much as I was interested in Kate's symptoms, I wasn't up to reading *The Johns Hopkins Medical Handbook*. I preferred to "hear" important information from real people rather than read it. So I called Dr. Barry Bowdoin, a marvelous buyer of illustrated books from the eighteen-nineties and my medical guru. He wasn't answering. I got his service instead. I left my name and number and asked him to call. "It's important," I told the man on the other end of the phone.

"I'm sure," he replied flatly.

I went back to the bedroom. Kate shut the *Handbook* and put it on the floor next to her bed. "I'm frightened," she said. Her voice had the timbre of a little girl's.

I went around to her side of the bed and sat next to her. I held her body in my arms. "You have a right to be," I said softly. "Cancer's a scary business." I stroked her hair with my fingers, pushing it off her forehead with a brushing motion. It was the first moment I had allowed myself to realize Kate could die from this. A new wave of panic washed over me. It was so strong, I thought for a moment I was going to lose consciousness.

"I don't know what's going to happen next," I heard Kate say from somewhere far away.

As rapidly as the panic had come, it disappeared. I held Kate's face in my hands and looked straight into her eyes. "We're together."

"Nice," Kate said without much feeling. She put her arms around me and we held each other closely. "I appreciate your being here," she said into my shoulder. "I really do."

While I held her, I wished there was someone there to comfort me. Despite my outward calm, my stomach had knotted with cramps and I felt I was on the verge of throwing up.

Chapter Three

Tuesday morning was chaos. It started with a call from Keith Stanley about the Jefferson letter. "Looks good!" Stanley reported.

"Not a forgery?"

"It's on eighteenth century French paper, written with eighteenth century ink. I must have handled two hundred Jefferson letters in the last ten years; the writing's his. What else can I tell you? It looks good enough to me." He hesitated, "Why? You have reason to think it's bogus?"

"Not really. Just some odd circumstances with the people offering it to me. I wanted to be sure is all."

"Well, it's got my good housekeeping seal of approval. In fact, if you buy it, please offer it to me."

I laughed. "Is it ethical for an appraiser to suggest such a thing?"

"Hey, I sell autographs," Stanley said. "I don't sit on the Vatican Council."

Alida Pendragon had been in the shop during the call. She had come early to look at a group of illuminated manuscripts and books illustrated by English women in the middle of the nineteenth century. They were beautiful and of substantial artistic merit. This was a socially acceptable art-form for gentlewomen to pursue in Victoria's England, but the male-dominated art world of the time largely dismissed it. While some of the chromolithographic books were actually sold by mainstream publishers, the women's husbands were usually asked to underwrite their production costs. In the minds of the arbiters of taste, paying to have these books published cheapened the endeavor.

Nevertheless, the art these women produced fascinated me. No one else I knew shared my passion, a precarious situation for a bookseller, but Alida sat on a stool in Parker's Rare Books looking carefully through my core collection, page by page, as I enthused in the background. Hope springs eternal!

"Dr. Bowdoin!" Bruce shouted to me from across the room, holding the telephone receiver over his head.

I went to the telephone on the counter and told Bowdoin about Kate's medical news. There is little privacy in a bookshop, at least in mine. As I looked up, I saw Alida Pendragon staring at me with a childlike, guiltless intensity.

"So?" he asked.

"So, what happens next?"

"Next, she gets the ultra-sound."

"And then?"

Barry Bowdoin sighed. He didn't like talking medicine to the unwashed. "Then, she gets the results." He had a medical school sneer in his voice.

"Barry, be patient! I have very little experience with ovarian cancer."

He laughed. "Don't put yourself down. In you I wouldn't expect first-hand knowledge." Then his voice lowered into a serious, more professional range. "Brad, there's a lot involved here. The doctor found a mass inside Kate. It could be cancer. It could be nothing."

"Nothing?"

"Well 'something,' but not cancer. In any case, the ultra-sound could tell you what it is. On the other hand, it could keep you guessing."

"Jesus, I'm glad we're having this talk!"

"Hey! You asked! Cancer's a complex business! It can't be explained in a sequence of sound bites."

"I'm sorry," I said. "Go on."

"Well, the ultra-sound will tell you how big the mass is and it will tell you if there's matter inside, or if it's mostly liquid."

"Meaning?"

"Simply put—matter is bad, liquid is good. If it's liquid, it's probably a cyst. Nasty, but you just remove it and go about your business. Now, even if it's 'matter,' it's still not time to panic. A mass in the general region where Kate has her's can grow to immense size and still not be cancerous. You following?"

"Yeah."

"My first lesson," Barry Bowdoin said. "You owe me a dinner at Cafe Bayou. Call me after the ultra-sound and we'll talk some more. It's sort of like phone sex. If I can get you to make enough calls, I might end up with a free trip to Paris."

I grunted into the receiver.

"One free piece of advice," Bowdoin continued. "Go with her to the doctor's office. When you're in the middle of something like this, there's a lot of information coming at you all at once. Two people have a better chance of digesting what a doctor tells them than one. It also doubles your chances of asking the right questions."

"Which are?"

"Depends on the circumstances and what they find. You'll know, and if you don't, for a price I'll tell you."

"For a price?"

"Hey, we are in the era of for-profit medical care. Aren't we?"

Out of the corner of my eye, I saw Peter Mosley walk into the shop. He wore an expensive looking sports jacket with an intricate patterned weave. His shoes were highly polished loafers with tassels. His movements, short and abrupt, were out of place with his classic, casual clothes.

"Thanks," I said to Bowdoin. "Gotta go now. Customers are taking numbers."

I put down the receiver. Alida and Peter both walked toward me at the same time. I turned to Alida. I wasn't ready yet for Peter Mosley.

"What's this with Kate?" Alida asked.

I didn't get a chance to reply. Peter had planted himself less than a foot from my right shoulder. Alida gave him her best men-are-pond-scum look, but he didn't move.

I peered around for Abbe and saw her standing outside in a coat and scarf.

"We'll talk later," Alida said, repeating the pond-scum effect, this time from over her shoulder as she walked away.

"What can I do for you?" I asked Peter behind as much of an innocent, beguiling smile as I could manage.

"I want the Jefferson letter back," Mosley said slowly and with determination.

I could have asked "What letter?" but I would have been childish and obvious, and I have rarely been accused of being obvious. Instead, I asked, "Abbe's letter?"

"It's really my letter," Mosley corrected me. He tried to match my smile, but he only succeeded in baring his front teeth. "There's been a misunderstanding."

"No misunderstanding," I replied. "I bought the letter from your wife."

"But it wasn't hers to sell," Mosley said, his voice an octave higher and much louder than when he began. "It's mine!"

"Not according to the statement she signed," I said. "Let's ask Abbe. She's standing outside."

"There's no reason to ask her," Mosley shouted. "It's *my* letter!"

When Abbe first slid the letter across my desk, I had had a premonition something like this might happen. I opened the shop door and called, "Abbe, come in for a second."

She turned around. She was wearing oversized sunglasses and a scarf on her head, but there was no hiding the bruises and abrasions on her cheek, or her puffy upper lip.

I spun around to face Peter. "You do this?" I said, pointing to Abbe.

Peter stood with his hands on his hips like a Broadway impersonation of a Siamese king. "You're avoiding the issue! I came for my letter and I'm not going to leave without it!"

Now we were both talking in raised voices, loud enough to bring Bruce from the shipping room. I didn't really care much about buying one Jefferson letter, but looking at how Peter had hurt Abbe made me want to hurt him back, and you hurt the Peters of this world through their pocket book. "I have a signed agreement to purchase the Jefferson letter," I said, "and I have another document identifying your wife as the owner."

The fact I had taken such care to make a simple purchase gave Mosley pause. "She's a liar."

"I strongly disagree!"

Mosley seemed to have another thought. "And I think you're a liar, too! I don't think you have a signed anything."

"Oh, really?" I arched my left eyebrow and reached for a three-ring-binder I keep on the counter. "What's this then?"

Peter Mosley made a clumsy grab for the book, but he was too slow and too far away.

"Peter, get out of my shop," I said, putting the binder back on the counter. "You're making an ass of yourself."

"I'll show you 'ass'!" Mosley said. He threw a looping right cross, aimed at my head.

I wasn't expecting it, but he had telegraphed the swing so an eighty year old man on crutches could have slipped it. I bobbed my head backwards and caught Mosley's wrist in my hands as it passed. Then, I used Peter's momentum to get behind him, drawing his index and middle fingers over his right shoulder into an exaggerated

"Heil Hitler" salute. I had my other hand poised over his throat.

"Mother-fucker!" Mosley screamed in pain.

"Now," I said softly into his left ear. "I can either break your two fingers by increasing pressure, pull your shoulder out of its socket, or break your goddamned neck, Mosley." I stood still, letting him think about it. "But I prefer to walk you quietly to the door and throw you out of my shop. You're not welcome here anymore."

I was afraid I would accidentally break his arm, so I slightly eased the pressure on his fingers. We walked slowly toward the door. Bruce had it open when we got there. People stopped and stared. I didn't blame them.

Outside, I let go of Mosley's arm and stepped back quickly. I really didn't have to. Pain had dissipated most of Mosley's fight. He rubbed his shoulder and his fingers.

"You haven't seen the last of me," Mosley threatened. "I'm going to the police."

"Go!"

"Come on, Abbe," Mosley yelled through the door and began walking away.

I glanced around. Abbe stood still next to Alida in the shop. Alida's eyes were wide with anger; Abbe's were slits of defiance.

Mosley doubled back to the shop door. "Damn it, Abbe! Let's go!"

"She's staying here," Alida said. There was calm resolution in her voice.

"Keep out of this!" Mosley shouted.

"And if I don't, what are you going to do? Hit me?"

"Bitch!" Mosley screamed and stormed off alone in the general direction of the police station.

I just stood there, feeling good about defending my own shop and honor. I wouldn't say I felt as macho as Mike Hammer, although I will admit I had a primal male smile on my face. But deep inside, I knew, at fifty-eight, I was too old to be involved in a brawl. Peter Mosley was at least twenty years my junior. If things had gone differently, I could have been standing there with a broken jaw or a mouthful of loose teeth. Sometimes I worried myself.

Chapter Four

Before Peter returned with the police, Alida had taken Abbe Mosley across the walkway from Parker's Rare Books to Rustermann's Restaurant. Peter must have been very vocal and forceful because the policeman he had in tow was Captain Philip Norge, head of the detective division. Norge had almost blond hair, heavily gelled and combed straight back. He was about thirty-five and had a deep sun tan which sooner or later would turn his skin into leather. But right now he looked good. He wore a grey Armani suit, and I was told he lived in the Williamsburg Happenings, the cheapest apartment complex in town. It made for an interesting contrast.

Before coming to Williamsburg, Norge had worked for the Los Angeles Police Department in the West Hollywood Division. There were many rumors on why he left the excitement and glamour for bucolic Williamsburg. These ranged from divorce, to drug dealing, to O.J. Simpson putting out a contract on his life—the list was flexible and imaginative. When asked, Norge would only say he tired of the LA scene. It was as good a truth as any. I had only met Norge once, at a party in the mayor's house. I remember wondering at the time how long Williamsburg would hold his interest.

Norge and Mosley walked into the shop, Mosley raving about how I had stolen his valuable letter and attacked him. The last part of his charge brought Bruce out of his shipping room.

"Bullshit!" Bruce bellowed.

There were two middle-aged tourists browsing through the floral prints. They had already separated two images of roses from the stack and were just about ready to buy them. After Bruce's remark, I watched the shorter of the two nervously put the prints back. She picked up her Cheese Shop tote bag from the floor and motioned her friend toward the door.

Norge looked around the shop with bemused indifference, probably estimating potential sales and wondering why anyone would bother trying to make a living from this. He took a gold pen and a small, cheap, spiral-bound notebook from his inside jacket pocket.

"Bullshit," Norge repeated in a disinterested monotone, and wrote something in his book.

"Mosley attacked Mr. Parker," Bruce said, pointing at the offender.

This set off another of Mosley's tirades.

"Calm down, Mr. Mosley," Norge said. He turned to me. "Mr. Mosley alleges you have a valuable letter belonging to him."

I explained what had happened and showed Norge the papers Abbe Mosley and I had signed.

"Do you have any proof the letter is yours and not your wife's?" Norge asked Mosley when I had finished.

Mosley's face reddened. "Parker's a thief! He only offered my wife fifty-five hundred dollars for it!"

"Your wife's asking price."

"Bitch!" It was obviously one of Mosley's favorite words. This time, I didn't know to whom he was referring, but I really didn't care.

With each of Mosley's outbursts, I had noticed Norge's calm detachment thinning. "Mr. Mosley, I'm just about finished here. You want to prefer charges?"

"Yes. Goddamnit!"

The original print buyers had already left. Another customer opened the door, heard Mosley's last remark, and turned away. It was going to be an expensive morning.

"Fifty-five hundred dollars falls under grand theft," Norge muttered to himself, writing again in his notebook.

"And assault," Mosley added.

Norge twisted his face slightly, nodded, and kept on writing.

Bruce made a guttural sound in the back of his throat and returned to the shipping room.

Norge asked who else was present during the incident and I told him.

"One more thing," Mosley said as an after-thought, "What have you done with my wife?"

"She left," I answered simply.

"Where did she go?"

"I have no idea," I lied.

Norge put his notebook and pen back in his jacket pocket.

"Well??" Mosley said.

"Well what, Mr. Mosley?"

"Aren't you going to recover my letter and hold it for evidence?"

Norge looked back at me. "Sound's reasonable," he said with a nonchalant shrug of his well-tailored shoulders. "It looks like this is going to court anyway."

"Fine," I answered, "but the letter's not here."

This set off Mosley once again.

"Settle down," Norge said, as if he were training a dog. Then he turned to me and asked, "Where is it?"

I explained about the appraisal.

"Bring the letter over to the police station when it's delivered," Norge said.

"*I'll* bring it," Mosley interrupted.

Norge stared at Mosley with a look which could have turned a less arrogant man into stone. "Mr. Mosley, as soon as I get back to the station, I'm calling a judge for a restraining order prohibiting you from entering this shop until the ownership of the letter is adjudicated. Simply put, you come here again, I'll arrest you."

Mosley's eyes narrowed. "Of course," he said. "No surprise! You and the business community are in bed with each other." Mosley stood for a moment, no doubt pondering this conspiracy. "Alright," he finally said, looking intently at Norge, "but I'm holding *you* responsible." Mosley stuck his right index finger less than two feet from Norge's face. "And I'm going to expect results. Soon!" Finally, Mosley stormed out of the shop.

"Not my candidate for 'Miss Congeniality'," Norge confided after he had left.

"Nor mine."

"Doesn't have any children, does he?"

"None I know," I replied.

"Thank God for small favors," Norge muttered. He raised his index and third finger of his right hand to his forehead in a mock salute. "And remember, bring me the letter."

* * * * *

Before Kate and I went to the Williamsburg Community Hospital for her ultra-sound, we stopped at Rustermann's. I had already told Kate what had happened. Antoine, the owner, directed us to a rear booth in the vault room behind the bar. It was a small, intimate dining area, away from the main traffic. Alida stood when she saw us at the doorway. Abbe sat silently in the corner. Alida walked over and engulfed Kate in her arms. "Ultra-sound?" she asked.

"Yes."

"Well, as medical procedures go, it's not as painful or invasive as most, so I wouldn't worry. He going with you?" Alida nodded toward me.

"Yes."

Alida patted a chair next to her for Kate to sit on. "And when they make you wear the hospital gown, insist they give you two. Wear the second one backwards. You'll be better protected. Whoever bought the gowns ought to be shot. Probably was a sex pervert, or a woman who wears a size six. You're not as large as I am, so it might not be a problem, but demand two anyway. You'll feel better."

Kate laughed. "I will."

Alida Pendragon's ease with people was an aspect of her I had never seen before.

"And when you're finished, come over to my house for dinner." Alida sat there with Kate's hand between both of her's, obviously in control of the situation, and loving it. "You can even bring your friend," she continued, nodding in my direction again. Alida looked directly at me now. "Abbe will be there. She's decided to stay at my house for the next few days." Alida sounded both pleased and relieved by this.

"Good decision!" I said.

Abbe looked up at me. She still wore her sunglasses. "Did Peter come back?" she asked.

"With the police. For now, Peter insists on taking this to court."

"Oh God, I'm sorry." Abbe began to cry.

Alida reached over and put an arm around Abbe's shoulder. "Why are you crying? The first thing you have to learn, my dear, is to stop apologizing for your husband. It's really not your job."

Alida sat there like a mother hen, her left arm around Abbe and her right hand reassuring Kate.

"We have to go," Kate said.

"Don't rush," Alida replied. "The hospital will keep you waiting. No reason not to do the same to them. Now, about dinner!" It was more of a command than a question.

"What time?" Kate asked.

"Six-thirty. But come early so I can show you the house in the light."

Kate looked up at me, anticipating.

"Sure," I said.

"We'll be there."

* * * * *

At the Williamsburg Community Hospital, Kate said, "Alida's nice." Kate's eyes sparkled. I loved the ivory highlights in her brown eyes. "I think we're going to be friends."

"I think you already are."

"You know it's been a long time since I've had a woman friend," Kate said.

We were sitting in the Radiology Waiting Room. "What's so special about a woman friend?" I asked.

"Just somebody to share girl talk with." Kate looked up at me. "Men don't share, do they?"

"We don't share girl talk with each other."

"No, men have this testosterone thing. They're too competitive to really share their inner feelings."

"What makes you so sure we have inner feelings?"

"Point well taken," Kate said.

I looked around the room at the odd assortment of people who were sitting there, waiting their turn for medical attention, waiting for someone to diagnose and treat whatever disease was troubling them. There were two blue-haired old ladies, an over-weight black woman with four young children crawling over her, a college student slouched in a chair with a hard cast extending from his toes to his waist, and three emaciated men in their late seventies, with blank expressions and little resolve. There was also a man in the corner wearing a dark grey Brooks Brothers suit, white shirt, and striped rep tie. I could not think of another place anywhere in our society where all these people would otherwise assemble.

But at the moment, being face-to-face with sickness and death scared the crap out of me. Kate was about to have a simple ultra-sound procedure and already I had sweated through my shirt.

The ultra-sound took less than a half-hour. They allowed me to be with Kate. We were led into a semi-darkened room where Kate was asked to lie on a metal bed. A nurse squirted a thick gel on her stomach then rolled an instrument over the area with a round ball at the end, which reminded me of a large, computer mouse. All the while the nurse watched a television screen on which an image appeared.

"How does it look?" Kate asked.

"I just take the pictures," the nurse replied. She couldn't have been older than twenty-five. "Your doctor will give you the results."

"But...."

"Can't give you a blow by blow or they'd fire me, but everything's going well. Relax!"

The nurse worked deftly and efficiently, asking Kate to move from one position to another. Finally, she left for a few minutes and returned. "Back on your side," she ordered. "They want me to attack this from another angle."

When the nurse left for a second time to check with the Wizard of Oz-like figure I imagined in the room beyond, I went over to hold Kate's hand. "How are you doing?"

"I'm fine. I'm glad you're here with me."

It surprised me to admit it, but I was glad, too. Kate's illness had brought us closer together, at least for the moment. My reaction stunned me. Grateful for Kate's potential cancer? I really needed to do some hard thinking about what was happening between us.

Chapter Five

❧❧

Alida Pendragon lived in Kingsmill, "a gated community," as they state in their advertising. Kate and I stopped at a guard house and waited until a uniformed man found our names on a list attached to his clipboard. He checked them off and gave us a large printed card for our windshield, identifying us as outsiders.

I don't like gated communities, and I don't like the elitism and separation for which they stand. I don't like them the same way I don't like Rush Limbaugh. They both exclude and divide. Limbaugh gives voice to some of the worse characteristics in American society: racism, women and gay bashing, and general intolerance. Gated communities, on the surface, are more benign. The people living in them simply don't want undesirables cruising around their neighborhoods.

What they get, though, is a false sense of security. I doubt if Kingsmill's police would deter a professional criminal, or a Peter Mosley. But my views on Kingsmill aren't widely held. "Utopian" communities are thriving all across America. It's one hell of a paranoid world.

In the two years since I first met her, I had never been invited to Alida's house. Maybe, I had told her once how I felt about gated communities. In any event, her house was set on a cul-de-sac at the end of a long, sloping lane. My first impression was Alida's had to be the smallest house in Kingsmill. I estimated it at less than two thousand square feet. Most of Kingsmill's homes looked as if they could house a large, extended, oriental family, or, God forbid, a 'sixties hippie commune. Alida's was a single-story affair of light grey wood with a flat roof and two long sky-lights running back from the entrance. The sky-lights continued half-way down the length of her house. You could see them from the top of the road, but as you descended into her gravel driveway, they were hidden from view again.

Three steps rose from the ground to a small entry. The empty frame of what had been a church window hung against the left wall. To the left and right of the entrance, were two small storage areas. Alida stood at the open door.

"How was the ultra-sound?" Alida asked Kate.

"Not so bad," Kate answered.

They hugged, then went in. I followed.

The outside of the house was so Shaker-plain, contrast alone made the inside all the more spectacular. We walked directly into a long central hall leading to a large room at the back of the house. The hall was bordered on both sides by two recessed "moats" filled with white stones on which large potted plants were placed. Above were the sky-lights. There were two small rooms beyond the plants, one to the left and one to the right. They were visible from the central hall through vertical slats. Alida saw me looking at them.

"You can open the slats or shut them," Alida said, grabbing one, which rotated on a central dowel attached to the ceiling and floor. "Makes the whole front of the house my bedroom when I'm alone, or I can close off the bedroom for privacy if I have company."

At the end of the hall, was a large all-purpose room. A fireplace was set in the center of the far wall, fifty feet from the front door. There was a kitchen and dining area to the left, featuring a long counter, with cabinets above and below it, extending along the complete length of the left wall.

On the right side of the room, were floor to ceiling bookcases.

At a glance, I recognized a number of titles from Parker's. A small grouping of chairs surrounded the fireplace. On either side of the hearth were floor-to-ceiling glass windows and sliding glass doors. Through them, you looked out and saw a deck. Beyond it was woodland, bordered by two gullies sloping down to form a narrowing V until, at a place where they almost met, the indentations dropped into the muddy brown waters of the James River. There were trees everywhere.

A deer grazed at the end of the path. It certainly was bucolic, and isolated as hell if Peter Mosley decided to pay a visit. Alida must have sensed my thoughts. "Don't worry," she said. "My security system would make the FBI jealous. Abbe will be safe here."

"I don't even think he knows where I am," Abbe added.

"Abbe has a little suite downstairs," said Alida, pointing to a round stairwell in front of the bookcases.

"This is a beautiful house," I said.

"It was designed by Carlton Abbott."

"He's a local architect, isn't he?" Kate said.

"*The* local architect! This was the first house he designed on his own, back in 1972."

We had a light dinner of soup, salad, roast chicken and rice. Alida poured a wonderfully complex New Zealand chardonnay. At seven-thirty, I made noises about going back to the bookshop for an hour.

"I'll stay, if it's alright?" Kate said.

I agreed to be back by nine.

* * * * *

In my office, I began to attack a computer problem. Sitting there in semi-darkness, I stared at a list of book descriptions I was converting into Internet-readable text. My mind wandered. I thought of Kate. Our relationship was changing and evolving as fast as the cancer which might be inside her. In normal times, I would have insisted we talk about the problems we were having. I wanted to find out what I had been doing to repeatedly drive her away. But these were not normal times. Kate might have cancer, I might be the one to take care of her. I didn't know how good I would be, but I would try. I know all relationships constantly evolve, but ours seemed to be changing at the speed of light. How would each of us feel if Kate got seriously ill? In fact, how did we feel about each other right now?

In some ways it was a relief Kate and Alida were becoming friends. Outside of business relationships, neither of us were very close to people we could count on in emergencies. Both our families, and dreams of families, were long gone. Knowing Alida was there for Kate would take some of the pressure off. But on some very basic level, their new friendship also frightened me. I saw a primal bonding taking place between them, a sisterhood excluding all males. I resented this and my resentment confused me. It wasn't rational—it was visceral—and in a time of emotional turmoil, I needed to concentrate on the rational. Insecure thoughts in the dark of night were the last things I wanted to deal with.

While pondering all this, mechanically clicking on the computer's keyboard to reorder the text, I glanced up from the screen. I refocused my eyes and saw a man standing in the doorway. He was approximately twenty-eight, stood six-foot-two, had long red hair pulled back into a ponytail, and was dressed in a colonial costume.

"Yes?" I asked. I was usually careful about locking the door behind me, but at fifty-eight, I no longer counted on myself to always do the usual things.

"You can see me!" the man said.

There was something about his voice, wild and uncertain, which frightened me. I was alone in the shop. Adrenalin made me alert. "Of course I can see you," I replied. "We're closed. What do you want?"

"I... I... I...," the man stammered.

I stood up, and immediately tripped over a wastebasket next to my desk.

The man's eyes grew wilder. My next step inadvertently kicked the metal basket against a floor lamp, making a horrible clatter. I looked down for an instant at the papers and mess on the floor. When I glanced up again, toward the man who had been in the doorway, he was gone. I got to the top of the steps without kicking anything else and looked down the staircase. I didn't see him.

I went downstairs as fast as I could, turning on lights along the way. I checked the door. I had locked the knob but had forgotten to put on the dead bolt. Then, I stopped and listened. The shop was quiet. Gordon was sitting in the middle of the room, looking at me as if I were mad. I went into Bruce's shipping area and grabbed the aluminum baseball bat he kept there for God knows what reason. Then, I made a thorough search of the remaining rooms and closets. The man had probably left by the front door while I danced with the wastebasket upstairs, but I wanted to be sure.

Later, I told the story at Alida's.

"You never saw him before?" Kate asked.

"Colonial Williamsburg has an actor who plays Thomas Jefferson, but this wasn't him."

"Is there a stand-in?"

"I don't know. I doubt it. It's too good an idea for them to have thought of by themselves."

"Aren't we cynical!" Alida chirped from the kitchen.

"If you pay as much rent to CW as I do, you're allowed."

"Could it have been someone Peter sent?" Abbe asked in a quiet voice. "Someone to steal the letter?"

"Do you know anyone who fits the description Brad gave?" Alida's curiosity had been piqued.

Abbe shook her head. "I don't know any of Peter's friends."

"Probably because he doesn't have any," Alida shot back.

"Peter wouldn't have tried," I said. "He knew the letter was at the appraiser's."

"But maybe there's something more to all this, pressuring Peter into desperate acts," Alida commented.

"It's a possibility." Then I looked at Abbe. She was sitting on the corner of the couch in a fetal position. "Abbe, when you were in my office, you mentioned a stack of Jefferson letters. Do you still have them?"

"No, they're at the house."

"If they're yours, you should get them. They could be worth a great deal of money."

"How much?" Alida asked.

"Depending on content, a half million dollars. Maybe more." I said this as matter-of-factly as I could. These were large figures for a poor bookseller.

"Brad, could Peter have hired the man to rough you up?" Alida asked.

"If he were Peter's man, why didn't he just do the job? I was alone."

"Maybe he panicked!"

"Or maybe my masculine prowess scared him away!"

"Oh, I doubt it," Alida said.

"In any event, I have a strong hunch the man might have been an outpatient from Eastern State."

"The mental hospital? Why?" Kate asked.

"His voice. The wildness of his eyes. Something was very different about him. He was abnormally frightened."

"If you kicked a wastebasket at me, I'd be afraid too," Kate said.

"I'm a klutz, not a threatening person."

"*I* know," Kate said a little too quickly. "Did *he?*"

"Have you called the authorities?" Alida asked.

"And say what? Nothing was stolen; the locks weren't jimmied. What happened was a potential customer, dressed in his colonial costume, came into my shop after hours and I scared him away."

"I wouldn't take this so lightly," Kate said. "A man in costume?"

"Kate, in Williamsburg, costumed character actors sometimes out-number the rest of us."

"Amen," Alida concluded.

* * * * *

Later, Kate lay next to me, her head in the crook of my right arm.

"The man in your shop was frightening."

"I know. I was there," I said.

"What are you going to do about it?"

"Get the locks changed early tomorrow morning for one thing. I don't want anyone to be able to sneak in, at least until this thing with the Jefferson letter is resolved."

"First a Jefferson letter. Then a man who looks like Thomas Jefferson." She added, "Will you still have time to go with me to the doctor's office tomorrow?"

"Wouldn't think of missing it." I felt a lump harden in my throat.

"I don't want to keep you from the shop."

"The wonderful thing about having your own business is choosing the eighty hours a week you want to work." Kate smiled and snuggled closer, like a large, soft cat. I realized I would miss her terribly if she were gone.

Chapter Six

I started Wednesday morning looking at the library of a professor who had died. There wasn't much there of compelling value. There hardly ever is with academic libraries. Professors don't *collect* books, they *use* them, but there were enough interesting and off-beat titles to add a certain extra-scholarly texture to my stock. The Internet was bringing this sort of specialized book into vogue again. You no longer had to wait for a unique customer studying an arcane subject to stumble into your shop. Customers world-wide now found *you*. So I made an offer, and the professor's widow said "yes." I spent the next hour packing six hundred or so books into every available square inch of my Toyota Camry. Experience had taught me to remove books as soon as I bought them. Even the nicest people lifted a title or two to better "remember" the collector. It was my lot in life to take away temptation as quickly as possible.

It was eleven-thirty when I got to Parker's Rare Books. The plan was for me to pick up Kate for her doctor's appointment, but my car was filled, floor-board to ceiling, with the professor's library. The weight of the books lowered my car and made it look like a 'sixties hot-rod. I explained my dilemma to Kate, who agreed to drive.

Arriving at the shop after it opens always puts me in a panic. I feel as though I were on the back end of a treadmill, running to catch up. People think of rare bookshops as bucolic islands of peace in a noisy and disruptive world. They're not. They are a mosaic of interruptions and chaos. As a bookseller, you have to be focused, or crazy—one or the other—to survive. No doubt I'm a little of both.

While Bruce finished with a customer, I checked the sales book to find what had sold that morning. When we were alone, I told him about my visitor from the night before.

"Spooky," he replied. "How did he get in?"

"I don't know, but I'd appreciate it if you would get a locksmith here this afternoon to re-key the place."

"Good idea," Bruce said.

"Get two sets of keys, one for you and one for me."

"And none for our landlord!" Bruce had worked at Parker's long enough to read my mind.

"Not until this problem with the Jefferson letter is resolved."

Bruce's face became flush. "You think Mosley...."

"I have no idea," I interrupted. "But let's be cautious." I started to walk away. Then I had another thought. "You still friendly with Marge?"

"Marge? In CW's Personnel Office?"

I nodded.

"She's in love with me." Bruce smiled. Bruce was sixty years old and widowed, but rarely alone. He had a solid, Germanic forthrightness, both in his character and in his appearance. His round, honest, guileless face appealed to women. It was also a face customers felt they could trust.

"Does she love you enough to tell you if CW has an understudy playing the Jefferson character?"

"I'll ask."

I left my car keys for Bruce, who promised to get our part-time book-packer to lug the books up to my office for pricing.

Before I left, I was able to write three customers about books we had recently purchased. I tried to use tiny snatches of time wisely.

On my way out, I literally bumped into Orville Sachs. Orville had been a mailman since the time when they actually were called "mailmen," before our language had gotten "person"alized.

"Oooo," he cringed in mock horror. "The Hulk Hogan of Merchant's Square. Heard you physically threw a customer out of your shop yesterday, Mr. Parker."

"Orville," I said, "I really don't have time."

"Roughing up tourists can be bad for business," he chided, his words, a sing-song chant.

"Wonder what they would think if I threw a long-term postal employee into a holly bush?"

"No reason to get belligerent!"

"The mail!" I demanded impatiently. I held out my hands and he put a large stack of letters and catalogues in them. He looked defeated and hurt. "Really, Orville," I said trying to appease. "I'm running late for a doctor's appointment with Kate." I don't know why I said it. Orville Sachs had no idea who Kate Whitney was.

* * * * *

Dr. Sallie Hancock's office was filled with women, all kinds of women—every age, shape, and color. While I waited, I mentally added airports and libraries to my list of common melting pots in American society. At least, I thought, there were three institutions combating the Kingsmills of the world. Of the three, libraries were by far the least expensive and frequently the most satisfying.

Kate and I sat for a half hour in the waiting room and then fifteen minutes more in Dr. Hancock's private office. There were seven people working for her. One was a nurse. The remainder, clerical help. Her suite of rooms looked like an insurance company's branch office, which it had become. Modern American medicine! Finally, Dr. Hancock arrived. She was a thin woman, somewhere in her late forties. She looked tired. Her face was etched with vertical lines. She could have been a poster girl for the sleep deprived.

Kate greeted her as "Doctor Sallie," a name I didn't feel comfortable using, and introduced the two of us. Dr. Hancock sat down at her rolltop desk and tore open a large envelope with Kate's name on it.

"Give me a minute to read your radiology report. I haven't had a chance yet," she explained. When she finished, Dr. Hancock picked up the x-rays and clipped them to a light box. "I think the mass is a little larger than when I examined you," she said to Kate.

"Is it my ovary?" Kate asked.

"Could be. It's very hard to tell from this. Here!" Dr. Hancock called us over and showed Kate the x-ray, pointing to a black area. I can't speak for Kate, but I could have been looking at a NASA photograph of Mars and not have known the difference.

"Is it liquid or solid matter?" I asked. It was my only question, so I thought I'd throw it out.

"It's not a cyst," Dr. Hancock replied. "I was hoping it would be, but there's definitely matter inside."

"You think it's cancer, then." Kate's throat was so constricted, she could hardly get the words out.

"Not necessarily, but it's a real possibility. I have to tell you."

"What do I do?" Kate asked.

"If I were you, I'd get rid of it as fast as possible."

"Surgery?"

Dr. Hancock's head nodded.

"What about a biopsy?"

"If it's cancer, a biopsy would only cause it to spread, and even if the mass isn't cancerous now, it could always metastasize. The accepted procedure these days is to do a laproscopic operation and look around the area. If the surgeons suspect the mass is cancer, they'll remove it along with any other questionable tissue."

"And if they don't find cancer?"

"Then you say thirty Hail Mary's and treat yourself to a very expensive dinner. If it's not cancer, they'll just remove the mass and do a biopsy on it later to be on the safe side. But once they're inside, the surgeons will know in a very few minutes."

"Aren't there any other tests they could do short of surgery?"

"I wish there were."

Kate expelled a breath. I reached over to hold her hand. It felt as cold as polar ice. All three of us sat wordless. The small office seemed even smaller now. I tried to digest what Dr. Hancock had said.

Kate broke the silence. "When should I have the operation?" she asked.

"As soon as possible."

"But I have to prepare. I have a restaurant to run!"

"I know," Dr. Hancock sympathized.

"I can't just leave!"

"I wouldn't wait." Dr. Hancock's eyes drifted back to the report. "It's definitely growing, not a good sign in a woman your age."

"But Dr. Sallie, there's no time to think!"

Dr. Hancock put the report and x-rays back in their folder. "I'm sure it seems so. Of course you're welcome to get a second opinion."

We discussed options. Barry Bowdoin had explained the advantages of a cancer team over a general hospital staff. I mentioned his comment.

"He has a point," Dr. Hancock admitted. "VS Hospital is the best in the area if you want a team approach. Unfortunately, I don't have very good connections there."

"I might," I said. "May I use your phone?"

While Kate asked more questions, I called Bowdoin. Of course, I couldn't reach him. So, I left my name and the bookshop's number.

* * * * *

Kate eventually found a parking space in one of the free

Merchants Square lots. Parking was an acute problem in downtown Williamsburg.

Kate had become adept at the game of "Vulture," our local version of musical chairs. Drivers circled the lot, trying to be in a position to claim the next available space. Kate found one in less than two minutes.

"You're good at this," I told her.

"It's because I live a virtuous life," Kate explained.

I was glad to hear her laugh.

The shop was crowded when we got there. I went straight to the telephone to call Barry Bowdoin before the vortex of bookshop business engulfed me. I was able to get through to him this time, and I introduced him to Kate before I handed the telephone to her.

While Kate talked, I helped a couple who seemed to be in their late twenties. They were thinking of buying a large mezzotint print of horses being trained. It was eighteenth century, German, and the black tones had the deepest, most velvet texture I had ever seen. It was also expensive. Twenty-five hundred dollars was multiples more than the young couple had ever considered paying for a print to hang on their walls. I said the encouraging things about the very best items increasing in value over the years, and left them alone to decide.

While I had been doing this, Bruce wrote an order for Parke Hollingshed. With the Christian Historical Trust's seemingly unlimited budget, Hollingshed had become one of our best customers. He had been a historian working for Colonial Williamsburg before going to CHT.

I first met him shortly after I had opened Parker's Rare Books. At the time, Hollingshed had just finished graduate school and had a reputation as a "comer." He began working for CW, wrote a well-received series of articles on colonial American life, and started to gain national recognition. Soon, the inevitable happened. I call it the CW Syndrome. They hire stallions but end up using them only to pull around children's pony carts. It's disheartening to watch.

With Hollingshed, projects he once enthused over were put "on hold." I remember seeing him walking his St. Bernard through Merchants Square at night, alone, and obviously depressed. It's the way not doing the work you want affects some men.

Then two years ago, he came into the bookshop.

"CHT offered me a writing job," he told me.

"What do they want you to write?" I asked.

"A book. An honest-to-God, full-length book. They made a sensational discovery about Thomas Jefferson. It's all very secret and hush-hush. I had to take a vow of silence, but the important thing is they want *me* to write it. I'll be working directly for Theodore Jay."

I made an encouraging noise.

"Brad, what do you know about CHT?"

"The short history? It began at Harvard as a left-wing organization funding Head Start and self-help projects in the ghettos, got very wealthy from internet stocks, and turned conservative and religiously right. Theodore Jay is the President. I don't think they do much of anything anymore except the bare minimum to keep their tax exempt status."

"But Jay's not a murderer or anything."

"Not to my knowledge."

"Good! I couldn't work for a murderer, but I can't see anything wrong in an outfit with money," Hollingshed said. "I don't like the Falwell—Robertson religious right, but it's only two years. This is too good of an opportunity to pass up over politics."

"Can you give me a hint on what the book will be about?" I asked.

"No, except to say Theodore Jay made an important Jefferson discovery."

"Sleeping with another of his slaves, was he?"

"Bigger," Hollingshed answered, rolling his eyes. "If it's written properly, I could win a Pulitzer Prize!"

Hollingshed was serious. "Will you be moving to Boston?" I asked.

"No! The best part is CHT rented the Taliaferro-Cole house from Colonial Williamsburg. I'll be living there, rent free, until the project's completed."

"Nice," I said.

"It's marvelous! And Theodore Jay is moving to Williamsburg, too."

"Where is he going to live, the President's House?" I asked. I was joking.

"You've heard!"

"You're kidding?"

"He made CW an offer and they accepted. You know how the Foundation always needs money."

"It must have been a lot of money."

Hollingshed nodded. "I think it was."

And what Hollingshed had said came to pass. While CHT's move to Williamsburg might have benefitted the Foundation, for Parker's Rare Books, it was like winning the lottery. Jay and Hollingshed decided to form a library of colonial American reference books, two thousand titles, and they bought them through us. They also paid their bills promptly. The Christian Historical Trust was an account booksellers dream of having.

Now, with the imminent publication of Hollingshed's book, I was afraid the good times were coming to an end.

"I heard you finished your writing," I said to Hollingshed.

He beamed. "And the Christian Historical Trust is throwing a Halloween Party to celebrate." Hollingshed must have sensed or remembered something. "By the way, your invitation's in the mail. I took the last batch to the post office today," he added.

It was a quick recovery on his part. I had known people who had received their invitations a month before.

Bruce interrupted with a receipt for Hollingshed to sign. I looked around and saw Kate was no longer talking on the telephone. So I excused myself, and the two of us went up the steps to my office. Gordon lay asleep in my chair.

"Well?"

"Your Dr. Bowdoin got me an appointment with a Dr. Cipriano on Friday at eleven o'clock. It's in Richmond. Can you take me?" Kate asked.

"Wouldn't miss it."

Kate leaned over and kissed me. From the corner of my eye I saw Gordon stir. He didn't seem to approve of physical contact between human beings. "Thank you for being there," Kate said.

"It's what it's all about."

Kate hugged me again.

When we went back downstairs, I saw Bruce writing up an invoice for the mezzotint print. The young couple was buying it after all. I congratulated them and meant it. I wished them the very best with their lives. It was then they told me they were on their honeymoon. If I had known, I would have given them a discount.

When we were alone Bruce said, "Ka-ching," making a sound like a cash register.

"It's going to be a good day," I agreed.

* * * * *

The business part of late lunch at Chez Bayou took up much more time than usual. Kate explained her imminent surgery. Then Napoleon, Chili, and Kate discussed how they would cover her work-load until she returned.

Napoleon asked Kate questions about her pending operation; Chili mostly pouted. While this was happening, I opened the mail Orville Sachs had handed me outside the shop. There was enough of a ratio of checks to bills to keep me happy. At the bottom of the pile, was a nine by twelve inch manila envelope from Keith Stanley. The Postal Service's green Return-Receipt-Requested card was still on the back. In the rush, Sachs had forgotten to have me sign it.

Inside me is a kernel of cussedness. I saw the envelope and thought of the bruises on Abbe's face. I followed Napoleon to the kitchen. "Could you keep this safe for me for a few days?" I asked.

He looked at the envelope and then at my face. There were dark, unspoken questions behind his stare, but "Course" is all he said.

"Be careful. It's valuable."

"Be safer than the crown jewels," he replied with a warm reassuring smile.

"And don't tell Kate!"

"Between us, bro."

I surprised myself, not wanting Kate to know. It was something to analyze.

* * * * *

Back in the office, Bruce greeted me with a grin. "Ka-ching," he said again.

"Now what sold?"

"The nineteenth century illuminated books. Miss Pendragon called. She wants them all."

"Mamma told me there'd be days like this."

Suddenly, Bruce's mood darkened. "Yes, but where are we going to find great books to replace them?" Bruce would have found something to be depressed about in the Garden of Eden.

I was making my escape up the stairs when I heard Bruce. "And before I forget," he shouted. "Marge at Colonial Williamsburg said they don't have a Jefferson understudy, and no one who works there even vaguely resembles your description of the visitor."

Chapter Seven

On Thursday morning, Kate was distant and inaccessible, temporarily a prisoner of her fears; she had circled the wagons and I was on the outside. Experience had taught me the best thing I could do now was get out of her way.

Once when Kate had been readying Chez Bayou for the public, she had gotten angry at something Chili had done, but she wouldn't talk to anyone about it for a week. All she did was to bark out orders like a marine drill sergeant.

The storm clouds were over everyone close to her, including me. I remember doing or saying something—I can't recall what now—ending in Kate not speaking to me.

"Jesus, what did I do?" I remember asking Napoleon.

"Oh, it's just Kate," Napoleon had said.

"Yeah, but she can keep the mood going for weeks. When it happens, living with Kate is like being alone," I continued venting. "No! It's worse!"

Napoleon sat next to me. "Brad, you and me, we lucky. We're open with people. If something bothers us, we can talk about it. Not Kate. Most of the time I don't think she even knows what's bothering her. Something happens, ain't important in the scheme of things, but it reminds her of an unhappy moment from her past. You live with Kate, you got to be prepared to live with her ghosts, too."

"Ghosts? Try, 'demons!'"

"The word don't make no difference," Napoleon said. "Only problem is she can hurt people when she gets like this."

"You're telling me!"

"Rule number six in my book of successful management," Napoleon continued, "is to get your ego out of the line of fire."

"Sometimes I think I'm in too deep," I remember saying.

"I know. And it's hard to ease back."

"It is if you're me."

"Then try being somebody different!"

* * * * *

In the morning, I did what I always do in times of stress, I left for the bookshop. Bookshops are wonderful inventions. They can take as much of your time and energy as you are willing to give and still ask for more.

I had come to bookselling by way of the CIA, which I had joined as a young soldier in Vietnam. It was to be a two-year break before graduate school; I stayed until I was in my late forties. My specialty had been cleaning up other agents' messes. I was very good at it. Once the President of the United States held a ceremony awarding me the Freedom Medal of Honor in the oval office at one in the morning. What I did to merit it was so secret I couldn't tell anyone. I handed back the award. It was placed in my employment file, never to be seen again.

I stayed in the agency until the year after my wife, Phyllis, died. She had been driving on the beltway around Washington when her car swerved and struck a concrete bridge pillar. My two boys were in the back seat. I lost my entire family.

I had lived in a state of shock for most of the following year. Then I really fell apart. I was assigned to a desk job at Camp Perry, where I could be properly watched. The CIA did not have an enlightened view of mental health, so when I went into therapy, I knew I had sealed my fate and had ended my career. Eventually,

I took my retirement funds and opened a bookshop in Williamsburg, Virginia. I began a life of buying and selling rare books. More than anything else, bookselling renewed my love of life.

In the morning, I had planned to add two large catalogues to our web site. I had been putting off the project because I knew it would take four hours of uninterrupted effort, but Kate's mood had rekindled my Protestant work-ethic. The truth was, without Kate, I couldn't think of anything better to do with my time, and I reasoned, for the moment, I had a better chance of "interfacing" with my computer than I did with her. I had noted a growing similarity between computers and women in my life, and was having a difficult time with both.   As with all bookshop plans, my latest was also subject to change. At ten-thirty there was a rap on my office door and Theodore Jay stood there smiling. "Like you to meet someone," he said. "Brad Parker, this is Rutherford Talon."

Rutherford Talon emerged from behind Jay and walked past him with his hand outstretched. "Glad to meet you," Talon said, and looked as if he meant it.

"Mr. Talon," I responded, extending my hand.

"Friends call me Ford."

"Mr. Talon is a candidate this year for Chairman of the Board of the Christian Historical Trust," Jay explained. Theodore Jay was both the current President and CEO. I didn't know enough about inside politics at the Trust to form any conclusion about Jay and Talon's relationship.

Talon was a big man, six-foot five, with a large frame like Napoleon's. He was a presence. Talon shook, or rather, enveloped my hand. His grip was firm, but unlike some men his size, he didn't squeeze or make handshaking a test of wills. Talon's hands were rough, no stranger to physical work.

At five-foot-eight, Jay was a sharp contrast. While Talon's features were roughly sculpted, with sharp and acute angles, Jay's were delicate. Jay looked like a woodblock illustration I had once seen of Cotton Mather, the early-American preacher. They had the same facial lines and the same festering, dour intensity. Somewhere, in Jay's case, his gene pool had added Richard Nixon's jowls and a perpetual five o'clock shadow to the mix. It was unfortunate. Many people didn't like him, but I did. Toward me, Jay had always been an honest and generous man.

"Nice place you got here," Talon said, looking around the shelves. "Have any books by or about Thomas Jefferson?"

"In Williamsburg?" I said. "There are several shelves of them downstairs in addition to what we've sold to the Trust."

Talon's face was blank.

"For the book Parke Hollingshed's writing on Jefferson," I prompted.

"One of our on-going projects," Jay quickly added. As he spoke, I saw a slight shudder ripple through his body.

"A book on Jefferson?" Talon asked.

"It was meant to be a surprise," Jay answered, "knowing how you love Thomas Jefferson."

The tension between the men was evident now, and my mentioning Hollingshed's book hadn't helped. I felt like the kid who opened his Christmas presents a week early.

"What's it about?" Talon asked.

"We discovered a special group of unpublished letters," Jay said.

My head snapped toward Jay like a pointer's to a duck.

"We've been keeping the exact nature of them a secret. Espionage in academia is worse than it is in the corporate world."

"I'll be damned," Talon said.

"You'll have a copy in less than two weeks," Jay promised.

A flash of anger washed over Talon's face and then was gone in an instant. I pegged him as a man who wanted everything and wanted it now. I wondered how he would have reacted to Jay if I wasn't present. For now, his smile returned. It was a practiced smile keeping hidden what was inside. "Two weeks then," Talon said, arching his eyebrows individually, first his left, then his right. He turned to me.

"Look forward to seeing you at our party," Talon said. "We've taken enough of your time. Come on Theodore, let's go downstairs and look at the man's books."

I followed them down the steps, showed Talon where our Thomas Jefferson section was, and watched him reverently remove several of the books from the shelf. You can tell a lot about a person from the way he handles books.

Out of the corner of my eye, I noticed two huge men leafing idly through the prints. Each was larger than Talon and more overtly muscular.

Talon must have seen me look. "They're with me," he said vaguely.

I was starting back upstairs, when Peter Mosley caromed into the shop.

"Where is the lying son-of-a-bitch?" he screamed.

Peter Mosley was staggeringly drunk. I looked over at Bruce, who already had the telephone receiver to his ear, hopefully dialing the Williamsburg police.

I walked to the print case in the center of the room.

"There you are," Mosley bellowed. "Where's my Jefferson letter?"

Both of Talon's men straightened and turned to face Mosley.

"Peter, go home! You're drunk," I said.

"You stole my Jefferson letter! I want it back!"

"It's not here," I told him. "Now go home before the police come. We've already called them."

Then Rutherford Talon asked, "Having trouble with this man, Mr. Parker?" He made a quick hand motion and his two friends took a step toward Mosley.

"No," I replied calmly. "Mr. Mosley was just leaving."

Peter Mosley suddenly became aware of the three monoliths

standing close by, staring at him. "Yeah," he said derisively. "You have your army around you now, but soon I'll find you alone. Then we'll see how brave you are."

"Goodbye, Peter," I called after him as he walked out the door, taking the tension of the room with him.

"What's his problem?" Rutherford Talon asked.

"A very long story about a Jefferson letter his wife sold me. They're going through a divorce."

"I went through a divorce once," Talon told me, shaking his head. "It messed me up for ten years."

* * * * *

Back in my office, Jay appeared in the doorway.

"We'd be interested in your Jefferson letter," Jay said.

"We?"

"The Christian Historical Trust. Rutherford Talon, too," he added.

"I'll keep you in mind, if it ever becomes mine to sell."

"Problems?"

"Peter Mosley and his wife disagree as to who owns it. We might have to go to court to settle the matter."

During a pause, I was able to ask my question. "Did you buy your Jefferson letters from Mosley?"

Jay stared searchingly at me. "What?"

"Abbe Mosley thought he sold some to the Trust a couple of years ago."

Jay shook his head. "No! Never bought anything from Mosley. The man has a bad reputation." Jay stopped and seemed to digest his answer.

"Who did you buy them from?"

"I promised not to tell. Part of the agreement, but if your letter does become available, I would love to buy it to commemorate the completion of Parke's book."

"Look, I'm sorry I mentioned the project."

Jay waved his hand in front of him. "Not to worry. You couldn't have known the situation." Jay paused and added, "I know I've taken an overly protective stance toward Parke's book, but it's worth all my efforts. The book is going to be a great success." Jay shifted his weight nervously from one leg to the other. "In many ways, I'm glad Talon knows." Jay was quiet. He had nothing more to say. So, with a perfunctory nod, he left.

Jay was surprisingly ill at ease for someone who did so much public speaking. His shyness was contagious, leaving me feeling like an awkward mute. Jay was nice enough, but he hid behind formality, probably to keep from getting hurt. A stray thought occurred to me: I wondered if anyone had ever called him "Teddy."

* * * * *

My next interruption was Detective Philip Norge, who came a half hour later.

"I heard you had a visitor," he said.

"I think Peter had a little too much to drink."

"The man's definitely crazy."

"Going through the first stages of divorce."

Norge waved some papers he was holding. "Mosley's summons."

"Mosley still wants to go through with this," I said.

"I tried to talk him out of it. I told him he could reach a reasonable agreement with you."

"What did he say?"

Norge shrugged his shoulders. "He thinks we're both part of a sinister conspiracy against him. Anyway, he has two weeks to mull it over," Norge pointed to the date on the summons. "In my opinion, he's mostly reacting to his wife leaving. He'll calm down."

"I hope so."

"And if he doesn't, from what I've seen, I think the judge will throw him and his case out of court."

* * * * *

In the evening, Kate stayed at the restaurant, which left me alone for a deli take-out sandwich at my desk. Finally, I was able to finish my work on the web site. Then, I began pricing the newly purchased professor's library.

Pricing books is an art form. The goal is to come up with the highest price for which a book will speedily sell. For twentieth century books, I create an imaginary bell-shaped curve to represent the market-place. For desirable architecture books, and books on colonial Virginia, my prices tend to be higher than most. I have private customers for these books, ones who don't have the time or inclination to shop around. For their loyalty, I quote new arrivals I think might be of interest. Because I'm willing to pay a fair price for books, I see a lot more unusual ones than anyone else I know, so my customers get first chance at the desirable rarities, books the tire-kicking bargain-hunters rarely see. I put lower prices on the more common also-rans, and very low prices on books outside my areas of expertise. I put very, very low prices on items I shouldn't have bought in the first place. Sometimes I price them for less than I paid, just to get rid of them. There's nothing worse for me than coming into the bookshop every day and staring at my mistakes.

My true love is the rare book, which appears on the world-wide market once or twice in a decade. Books like this bring happiness to a serious collector and personal joy for me. I get a chance to play God, placing the right volume in the right collection. These are books you'll never find on the World-Wide-Web.

I was pricing a fine copy of James Goode's *The Best Places* when I looked up and saw the costumed man again. He was standing in my office doorway. I had been expecting him. I casually opened the file drawer of my desk, where I had placed my Smith and Wesson.

"I need your help," he said. The strange tremor was still in his voice.

"Who are you?" I asked.

"My name is Thomas Jefferson," the man said proudly.

I reached down and put my hand around Smith and Wesson. "Thomas Jefferson has been dead for over a hundred and seventy-five years," I replied in an even, quiet tone. I didn't want to excite him. I had even placed my wastebasket away from the desk so I wouldn't accidently kick it.

"I have been dead for those many years, too," the man replied.

"Look, I don't know what your problem is...."

"It's the letters. My problem is the letters."

He took a step forward. I brought the Smith and Wesson out of the drawer and pointed it at him.

"Stay right where you are," I ordered. My voice quivered. My throat was dry with tension.

"But you don't understand."

"Understand what?"

His eyes were deep and empty. "I'm not alive."

"You won't be if you take another step," I warned him. God, I didn't want to shoot this man!

He opened his mouth to speak, his eyes were troubled, anguished really. "You don't understand," he repeated. "I'm a spirit." He held out his left arm parallel to the ground and turned around. His arm went toward the wall, then through it. He stood again, whole in the doorway.

I don't know how long I sat there, mouth open, gun pointed at the figure. I could have shot him. I think a jury of my peers would have found me innocent, but I didn't want to be known as the bookseller who shot a magician playing a prank, and I was reasonably sure there was some similar explanation behind what I was seeing.

"We've talked enough tonight," Jefferson said abruptly. Then he turned and walked into the wall. This time his entire body was absorbed by it and he did not reappear. Except for me, the office was empty.

My mouth was still open. I half expected to see the new Allen

Funt and his *Candid Camera* crew, but no one came. I laid the gun on my desk and looked down at my right hand. It was trembling.

I heard a slight noise on the steps. I tensed and picked up the Smith and Wesson again. "Who's there?"

Gordon appeared.

"Damned cat! Where were you when I needed you?" I asked.

Gordon mewed in response, reminding me I had not fed him. "I must be crazy," I said out loud. "First, I'm talking to a ghost. Now, a cat."

Gordon turned and left. My last remark must have offended him deeply.

Chapter Eight

⊱✿⊰

After I checked downstairs, my encounter with Thomas Jefferson began reacting on me like a jalapeno pepper. This time I *had* remembered to lock the dead bolt; this time I had searched *all* the cubby-holes, anyplace even a double-jointed human being could squeeze, and still, I couldn't find my costumed prankster. I checked above the dropped ceiling. Nothing. And Gordon was not sniffing near any odd places either.

Baffled, I sat on top of the print case. There was no way Thomas Jefferson could have gotten out of the shop and yet he definitely was not inside. Then... My God! What if I had just imagined him? He seemed so real, but psychotics thought their visions real, too. What if Thomas Jefferson was only in my mind?

I had never had an hallucination before, and I wasn't ready to admit I had had one then. I'll confess—yes, there was stress in my life, what with the business, the Mosleys, Kate's illness. I had been feeling tense, but I thought I was handling it with grace if not ease. Maybe I wasn't.

I couldn't afford the luxury of losing my mind. But there I was, standing in the middle of my bookshop, thinking about hallucinations, ghosts, and reality. Just where was the borderline between sanity and these flights of fancy? Before, when I had suffered a breakdown after losing my family, stress had caused a long, deep depression, but even at my worse, I didn't see visions. Why would

I be seeing them now?

Gordon burrowed his head between my arm and side with increasing frustration. Finally, I got up and opened a can of cat food for him. At least in Gordon's eyes this act made me an acceptable human being again. It didn't take much to regain his admiration.

* * * * *

I didn't have time to dwell on Thomas Jefferson or fall apart over the state of my mental health. Kate met me at my apartment as I pulled in the driveway.

"Don't stop!" Kate said anxiously. "Alida called. She's worried! She needs our help!" Kate got into the passenger's seat.

"What's wrong?" I asked.

"Abbe! She went back to the house to pick up clothes. She left Alida's at four."

I looked at the clock on the dashboard. Eight-thirty. "Maybe the Mosleys patched up their differences."

"And maybe cows *can* jump over the moon!" Kate replied.

"Stranger things have happened." I was thinking of Thomas Jefferson.

"Alida went over to the Mosley's house. I told her we'd meet her there."

The Mosleys lived in a three-story Victorian farm house a half mile off Jamestown Road, mid-way between Williamsburg and the ferry crossing. Now, there was a subdivision where the farm used to be, but the old house still stood, hidden in a grove of tall pines and maples. I pulled into the dirt driveway and saw Alida's Volvo station wagon in front of me. I saw it clearly because it was silhouetted by flames coming directly from the house.

The entire one-floor addition, where Peter Mosley conducted his book business, was engulfed in searing white and blue flames. The front door was open. I could see billowing smoke inside.

Alida stood next to her car, a portable phone in her hand.

"You call the fire department?" I asked.

She nodded. "Abbe's inside!"

"Did you see her?"

"I know she is! I just know it. She was going to get clothes! Her bedroom's on the second floor!"

"Oh, shit!" I thought. I might have said it, too. I knew what had to be done and I knew I was going to do it.

I ran toward the house. I could feel the heat ten yards from the front door. I reached for my handkerchief to put over my nose—a useless gesture—and I reminded myself not to touch anything. I had burnt my hands once before, rushing into a burning building in Saigon, in my youth, in a time so distant it felt like another man's life.

The fire was roaring from the direction of Peter's study. I could hear crackling and glass breaking in the living room to my right. I didn't have much time. I took the steps in twos. Then at the top, I crept on all fours to see underneath the smoke.

Alida's premonition was right. Abbe lay on the floor in the middle of a bedroom. I could hear the fire downstairs. It had intensified. I thought the building might explode. I quickly grabbed a bedspread and put it around Abbe. I made one failed attempt at a fireman's carry, cursed myself for getting old, and dragged Abbe toward the stairs.

There was a crash below. Something had collapsed sending a puff of flame, like a dragon's breath, from the place where Peter's book business used to be.

I inhaled as deeply as I dared, grabbed Abbe firmly under her arms, and began walking backwards down the steps as fast as I could, dragging her behind me. I didn't stop until I was outside, off the porch, past the fire's deadly grip. Then I fell backwards onto the lawn.

Two firemen rushed towards us. I coughed and continued to cough. One of the fireman walked me back to a truck, where he gave me a plastic mask which was hooked-up to a supply of pure oxygen. I breathed and watched an ambulance arrive. Men put Abbe on a gurney and wheeled her toward it. Soon the ambulance doors were shut and it drove away.

Kate was at my side. "How's Abbe?" I asked.

"Unconscious."

"She was when I found her upstairs, too."

"Alida went with her to the hospital. How are you?"

"Fine," I said.

"You don't look it!"

I stared at my hands. They were not burnt but I could feel the remembered pain from the fire in Saigon over thirty years ago. I had lived almost half my life since then, but the searing pain in my hands and in my heart seemed just as real now as it had then.

My actions there had won me a Silver Star, but a Vietnamese woman, Mae Ling, whom I had loved deeply, had died in the blaze. The Silver Star just hadn't compensated for her. At the Mosley fire I realized, once again, my remembrances of Saigon would not go away. They could not be swept from my memory no matter how hard I had tried to forget. The fire in Saigon was etched inside me, a permanent wound from the War itself.

Chapter Nine

I was on overload. I had only slept for two hours before the events of the day jarred me awake. I sat bolt upright, sweating and breathing erratically. I went into the kitchen so I wouldn't wake Kate.

I had done it again, acted impulsively. I had run into a burning house to save someone I wasn't even sure was there, with only Alida Pendragon's "premonition" to guide me. I had risked my life. For what? A Silver Star? A Presidential Freedom Award? Jesus!

The only good to come from the fire was I hadn't been able to think about Thomas Jefferson. I was standing in the kitchen, trying to get a drink of water, but I couldn't bring the glass to my mouth because my hand was shaking so badly.

Maybe I *was* falling apart.

Kate might have cancer. Kate might die. And if she didn't, I knew viscerally Kate was mentally preparing to leave.

I sat on the floor in the darkened living room for the rest of the night, rocking back and forth like a patient from a mental institution. Was Jefferson, my friendly visitor, doing the same? At six o'clock, I stirred myself and went into the bathroom for a long shower.

"I didn't even hear you get up," Kate said when I had come out.

"Couldn't sleep," I answered.

* * * * *

Kate and I waited in the OB GYN/Cancer Clinic. It was in a building separate from the hospital itself. I sat next to Kate and read a copy of *People* magazine. *People* is one of my guilty pleasures. An eight-year-old black boy peered at us from around a corner. He had the devil in his eyes, ready to pop any second. I stuck out my tongue. He thought this was a fine game and returned the gesture, laughing. I heard a woman's scolding voice behind him and the boy disappeared.

Despite the reprimand, I was finding most people in hospital waiting rooms were unnaturally cheerful. They must have felt if they were nice to other people, God would notice and be kind to them. Sitting next to these happy faces were a few with vacuous stares, so lost in their own private fears they had disconnected from the real world, waiting only for their bodies to follow. I observed very few people who fell in between these extremes.

A few minutes later someone called Kate's name and we followed a nurse to a small cubicle serving as an office. She escorted us inside and closed the door on her way out.

"It's like waiting for a table at a good restaurant," Kate said. "You stand at the maitre d's station for a while and then they shift you to the bar."

"Makes you feel as if you're making progress."

"But you're still 'waiting.'"

"Still 'waiting,'" I echoed.

After a few minutes, the nurse came back and took Kate to yet another room for an examination.

Alone, I began to involuntarily shake like someone with malaria. It was a repeat of last night. I sat forward and hugged myself until I gained some control. I was having a bad reaction from rushing into the fire. I worried it was a death wish on my part, an unconscious urge to end my own life. In an instant, I had thoughts of Vietnam, Phyllis' auto accident, the deaths of our sons—so many undigested events in my psyche! But everyone has them, I concluded.

How many of us truly understand what has happened in our lives? And if we do, are we any better for the insight?

And then there was, never far from consciousness, my possible hallucination, Thomas Jefferson. Jesus! I had a right to be worried!

When Kate returned, we waited in the small office for an additional twenty minutes. The copy of *People* I had brought with me from the main waiting room had lost its allure.

Then a woman, who appeared to be in her early thirties, knocked and came in. She had short black hair cut in a bob and under the hair were glistening green eyes. She introduced herself to me as Dr. Cipriano. She was the one who had just examined Kate. Her movements were quick and assured without being brusque. I don't often use the word, but Dr. Cipriano was "perky," not an easy thing to be working twelve hour days. She was followed by a slightly younger woman, perhaps a student, introduced as Mandy.

Dr. Cipriano sat down at a small desk and looked over the x-rays and reports Kate had brought with her.

"Do you know if they used a doppler on the ultra-sound?" she asked Kate.

"I have no idea," Kate answered.

"They would have included a report if they did," Cipriano said, answering her own question.

"Maybe they don't have one," Mandy suggested.

"Williamsburg is a small hospital. Maybe they don't."

"What is a doppler?" I asked.

"Like the doppler effect of a passing train," Cipriano said. "In this case we get a reading from reflected waves which measure the flow of blood to the mass."

"What's the significance?" Kate asked.

"The more blood going through the mass, the greater the chance the mass is cancerous. By the way, did your doctor do any blood work?" Cipriano paged through the reports.

"No," Kate replied. "She said if she ordered it, the insurance company wouldn't pay."

"Well, I want you to have one. If *I* order it, they *will* pay, and if it's a good report, it will give you peace of mind. For me, a gushing flow of blood or a trickle, I'll still have to go in and take a look."

Cipriano described the operation. "We'll start laproscopically. I'll make three, small incisions," she said, pointing to her stomach, "and another in your belly button. It takes longer this way, but it's the difference between two weeks of recovery and six with a standard cut." Demonstrating, Cipriano drew her hand from a place just under her breasts to her navel.

"If anything looks obvious or even suspicious, I'll open you up and remove all the cancer I find. I'll also take biopsies of the major organs, so I'll need your written permission in advance."

Kate had become pale. "Things are moving fast, aren't they?"

"Once the operation starts, things, as you call them, will move *very* fast. We never know what we'll find, so we have to be prepared for everything."

"I've watched her. You're in good hands," Mandy said reassuringly.

"What if this is just a mass and it's not cancer?" I asked.

"Then we'll enclose it in a little sack. I'll cut it off and remove it. It's not good to let something grow inside you forever. With this procedure, using the sack, if the mass bursts, it won't come in contact with your other organs. It's a precaution. We'll biopsy everything after it's out to be on the safe side."

"If you're only making three tiny cuts, how will you get the mass out?" Kate asked. "I was told it's now the size of a small grapefruit and growing."

"We'll take it out by way of the lowest incision. I might have to enlarge one cut slightly, but an enlarged lapro-cut is still a lot better than traditional surgery."

"You think you can remove a mass this large?" Kate asked.

"Yes, I do. I have! I may look young, but I've been doing this procedure for eight years now."

I liked the way Cipriano answered. Her voice was filled with understated confidence, and she met Kate's gaze and held it through the following silence. I wondered if they taught poise in medical school.

Kate looked at me, then back to the doctor.

I wore my stoic, impassive face, the one I use when I'm making an offer on a library, but inside I was churning.

Kate took a deep breath and let it out in a sigh. "When can we do it?" Kate finally asked.

Cipriano took out an electronic daytimer and tapped at its keys. "How about Wednesday morning?"

"Next Wednesday? Five days from now?"

"I'm free. After I examine you, I'll reserve an operating room, and I'm confident my staff can get the approval from your insurance company by then." She glanced over the papers once more to double-check and then looked up. "I don't see a problem, and if I had your symptoms, I'd want the operation as soon as possible."

"It's what Doctor Sallie said, too." Kate sat quietly, then looked at me again. "Brad?"

"I don't think there's anything to be gained by waiting," I answered.

"Alright." Kate slapped her hands against her thighs. "Let's do it."

"And if you possibly can, go away somewhere together for the weekend. Keep your mind off the operation," Cipriano said. "But this afternoon, Kate, we still have some work for you to do."

Dr. Cipriano scheduled a battery of procedures: an EKG, blood work, x-rays—all to be done in the same building. While Kate was being probed, I went to a pay phone and called Alida's house. There was no answer. Then I got the telephone number for the Williamsburg Community Hospital.

"A patient, Mrs. Peter Mosley," I said to the operator.

There was a long pause. "Mrs. Mosley is in Intensive Care."

"May I speak to someone there?"

"And what is your relationship with the patient?" the operator asked.

"I'm her brother," I lied. I lied again to the nurse in the Intensive Care Unit. I asked what Abbe's status was. She said she didn't give information over the telephone. "Is anyone with her?" I finally asked.

"An elderly woman with white hair," she said.

I hoped for the nurse's sake Alida didn't hear the remark.

Finally, Alida was at the phone. "Brad, she's still in a coma. How's Kate?"

"Scheduled to be operated on next Wednesday." I told Alida about our appointment with Dr. Cipriano, including the suggested weekend vacation.

"If you're asking my permission, you have it," Alida said. "There's nothing you can do here. Your responsibility is to Kate. Take her away and be good to her."

"Are you sure you'll be okay? You sound very depressed."

"It's just Abbe's bad timing. Her bad luck. Do you know how Peter knew the letter was missing?"

"No," I said.

"The same day Abbe saw you was the one Peter picked to check all the letters against an inventory he had made. While he was slapping Abbe around, he told her this to show how smart he was."

"Why did he check the inventory then?"

"He told Abbe he was about to sell them to a New York client." Alida added. "It surprised Abbe because she thought he had sold the letters to the Christian Historical Trust three years before."

"Theodore Jay told me the Trust didn't buy their letters from Mosley."

"Abbe thought they did!"

"If it's true, the letters weren't hers to sell, after all."

"If they were Peter's, half belonged to Abbe," Alida reminded me. "It's the way the law works in this state!"

When we finished talking, I dialed the Sanderling Inn in Duck, North Carolina, on the Outer Banks. They had just had a cancellation, so I reserved the newly available room for the weekend.

Finally, I called Bruce at the shop. "Captain Norge is looking for you," he told me. "I said you were at VC Hospital with Kate. From his reaction, I wouldn't be surprised if he sends a posse to bring you back."

"You know what he wants?"

"They found a charred body in the fire last night."

"Christ! Whose?"

"The newspaper didn't say. I don't think they know."

"Where was the body found?"

"In Peter Mosley's office."

I remembered the searing heat from Peter's wing. "I'm not surprised they couldn't identify the corpse."

Bruce paused. "The newspaper mentioned your name, by the way. According to them you're a local hero."

I groaned.

"I'm waiting for Wheaties to call. If they want your picture on a cereal box, how much should I ask for?"

"Not funny." I wondered again what exactly had happened in the Mosley house. I thought about the open front door. "Bruce, can you cover for me at the shop this weekend?"

"Yeah, but Norge seemed very insistent on talking with you. Where are you going?"

"If I don't tell you, you won't know."

"And won't have to lie."

"Precisely." We went over business details for another five minutes.

* * * * *

The hardest part of the weekend was convincing Kate she should go.

"Doctor's orders," I reminded her.

She looked at me with a bemused glance. "Since when did you ever follow doctor's orders?"

I looked down at my wrist where a watch should have been, but wasn't. "Oh," I made a calculating grimace, "Thirty seconds ago?"

"Exactly!" said Kate.

"I thought I'd give compliance a try."

"Brad, I have the restaurant to run. And then there's Alida and Abbe!"

"Alida has given you her papal blessing for a two-day vacation."

"You spoke with her?"

"At the hospital. Abbe's still in a coma. There's nothing you can do there, and your two partners seem to have Chez Bayou under control."

Kate sighed. "I do need a couple of days away." I was glad because the reservations I had made at the Sanderling were non-refundable.

I still possessed subtle and remarkable powers of persuasion. I remained a silver-tongued devil.

Chapter Ten

❦

On the North Carolina coast, Kate and I stopped for dinner at The Blue Point in Duck, two miles down the road from the Sanderling Inn. The decor was nineteen-fifties-diner with tables outfitted with formica tops and aluminum bands along their sides. The chairs were chrome and vinyl. While the look was retro, the food was not. I had soft shell crabs, sauteed, and served with a spicy mango chutney. There was a side dish of cole slaw, at its center a nest of very thin, deep-fried curls of beet. Kate had crab cakes made without egg or mayonnaise to bind them. The patty was held together by magic. With the lump crab meat, was a tangy seasoning which complemented but did not overwhelm the taste of the crab itself. The crab cakes were a house specialty and earned the restaurant an extra star in the Mobil guide. The Blue Point's promotional folder, on each table, also touted the fact it was one of only three restaurants listed by Zagat for North Carolina. Zagat had rated the place at twenty-six, a very high mark in their scheme of things, especially for a glorified diner with extras.

Tommy Glanville, a graduate of the Culinary Institute of America, was the chef. He came from Williamsburg and had worked for a short while at Rustermann's, which is where we met. Of course, he collected cookbooks. Tommy had not been happy working for Antoine. He had a burning desire to have his own restaurant. It was his obsession and it made working for others a form of slavery.

When the opportunity came to start The Blue Point, he had made the most of it.

Tommy arrived at our table when we finished our entrees. He offered complimentary after-dinner drinks, and we accepted. The talk was about Williamsburg and how Chez Bayou was faring. Kate was fine when Tommy first sat down, but I noticed her becoming increasingly quiet as Tommy launched into one of his long stories.

"You okay?" I asked Kate when Tommy had gone.

"No!" Kate answered. "I'm going to have a very serious operation on Wednesday. I might have cancer! I might die! No, I'm not okay! I'm scared out of my mind!"

I reached across the table and put my hands over hers. "Let's get out of here." I paid the bill and we left. Kate and I stood in the dark next to her car for at least twenty minutes, my arms around her. All I could do was hold her. Ultimately, Kate had to deal with the panic attacks from within herself.

* * * * *

I had gotten closer to Kate than to anyone I had ever known, including my wife, Phyllis. I shared my successes and failures with Kate, my highs and my lows, and, to a great degree, she shared her life with me. I remembered a lunch we had had at Louie's 106 in Austin, Texas, when we were just getting reacquainted.

"Back when Phyllis' accident happened, I was devastated," Kate had said.

"I remember your note."

"I'm sorry I wasn't there for you. The four of us were so close when we were young. But then, I wasn't there for anyone, including myself."

"A lot of pain," I agreed, and then for some unknown reason, I started talking about Phyllis' car crash, about the void, about the thousands of little decisions I had to make by myself, about feeling so terribly alone. I probably talked for twenty minutes or more. The words gushed out of me. In all the time since the crash, I had never really talked to anyone about Phyllis' death.

Finally, I reached into my wallet and handed the note to Kate. "I found it ten months after the accident. I was cleaning the bedroom closet. It was lying inside a box where we kept family pictures."

Kate started reading. Her face contorted. "She killed herself! My God!"

"And the children. She couldn't stand the barriers I had set between myself and the rest of the world and she saw these same traits in the boys."

"Oh, Brad! This is sick!"

"I had some leave coming and somehow got myself to the Outer Banks. It was the dead of winter. I rented a hotel room and just walked the beach, screaming at the surf and the wind. I was completely out of my mind."

"You blamed yourself?" Kate asked.

"For setting up the barriers between us, yes! The death of my wife and children was Phyllis's doing."

Kate appeared to be in shock.

"The next few months were terrible," I said. "I felt depressed, suicidal really. It didn't take long to get to a point where I was barely functioning. Then I started seeing a shrink, which led to my leaving the CIA."

"How did you survive?"

"I don't know, but I'm still here! Every once in a while, though, I have the nightmare, even now. It's the one where I'm sitting in our car. Phyllis is driving. We're talking about grocery lists, schedules, and Phyllis is driving faster and faster. I remember mentioning dental floss. Then, I look up. The overpass' support column is right in front of us. The boys are screaming for me to do something. The nightmare is a real winner!"

"And you never told your shrink about this?" Kate asked.

"I was ashamed."

"Of what?"

Tears had started running down my face.

"It's alright," Kate said. "It's okay."

* * * * *

We lay in bed at the Sanderling, listening to the ocean. A full harvest moon lit our room. I was on my back, Kate's head in the crook of my right shoulder. She slept fitfully. Occasionally her arm or leg would twitch inadvertently and she would mutter something I didn't understand. When she did stir, I would run my hand gently down her arm, which seemed to calm her. Whatever my touch did, at least she slept.

Me? I lay there with thoughts of Thomas Jefferson. I had seen him twice—both times in my office. I nervously looked around our hotel room, half-expecting him to be at the foot of the bed. I wondered if I could conjure up Thomas Jefferson here at the Sanderling, or did we only have conversations at the bookshop?

Stress! Depression! They were there. I remembered the signs from when I had found Phyllis' note. But I was coping better now. In fact, I thought I was handling life fairly well. I wondered if schizophrenics and psychotics felt they were doing well, too.

Kate moved to a fetal position on her side of the bed. I was sweating, worrying about being crazy, worrying about why I had run into the Mosley house, worrying about my fight with Peter. I was closer to panic then than I had been since finding Phyllis' note. I knew insanity would destroy the slender threads holding my life together: my relationship with Kate, my business.... How long could the business go on without me? Bruce was a fantastic employee, but I was the only experienced buyer. In two or three months, the stock would be in a pitiful state. Then there was a further question: would Colonial Williamsburg Foundation renew the lease of a crazy man?

Questions! I wondered how long it took to cure people like me? Was there a pill I could swallow, or would I have to be institutionalized? Eventually I would ask a doctor, but not now, not until after Kate's operation.

* * * * *

Sometime during the night I fell asleep. I woke to the sound of a shower. I patted the bed next to me for Kate, who wasn't there. I must have drifted to sleep again, because the next thing I saw was Kate sitting on the bed, drying her hair with a towel.

"Lazy-bones!" she said.

"What time is it?"

"Seven! Let's get breakfast and then take a walk on the beach."

Despite my lack of sleep, I felt refreshed strolling along the beach, watching the waves. For me the ocean is a primal reminder of where we all came from. Who knows? It could be just the rhythm of the waves, percussions for the soul, but when I'm at the shore, I feel connected to something larger and more important than myself. On good days, it was also true of bookselling, too.

Kate and I walked for three hours. She gathered blue beach glass from the sand whenever she saw a piece. Most of the glass pieces were tiny, smaller than a baby pearl. Kate had put her booty from past trips in a Mason jar which she kept on her kitchen window-sill. She liked the way sun reflected off the glass.

At six, we went back to The Blue Point in a vain attempt to eat our way down the entrees on the menu. We both copped-out and settled on bouillabaisse, the unprinted special for the day. I ordered a bottle of Sonoma Cutrer wine to go with it. We skipped dessert.

* * * * *

My sleep on Saturday night was better than the night before, but it was still fitful.

As I drifted off, strange disparate thoughts connected in my brain. I remembered an assignment for the CIA, a strange documents expert, Max Durgan, Saigon, Phyllis, and top secret work the agency was doing with holograms. In the middle of the night I woke. Could their research have resulted in Thomas Jefferson? The CIA was not above playing mind games on people.

All night, as a background to my uneasy thoughts, I could hear the ocean, the waves rhythmically pounding against the beach. In a half-world, between wake and sleep, the steady pulse of the ocean seemed to override my dark thoughts.

* * * * *

We left Duck at three on Sunday afternoon, and, yes, we ate lunch at The Blue Point before our drive back.

"The weekend was good," Kate said. "Now I'm prepared for what lies ahead."

"Not to mention adding a new layer of blue beach glass to your collection."

"Something I would never mention!" Kate laughed.

Her laugh warmed me.

Chapter Eleven

On Monday I got to the office at six-thirty to try to get ahead of the impending avalanche. The first day back from even a short vacation was horrible.

It took me an hour to take care of the shop's Internet business: orders, questions, e-mail needing replies—all the details making what I do a business.

At eight sharp, I dialed a number I had memorized many years before. It connected me with the CIA mailbox. An answering machine beeped and I left my name, telephone number, and password. Fifteen minutes later, my old supervisor, Max Durgan, called.

"And how may I be of service?" he asked.

I had almost forgotten the smarmy lilt of his voice, but I noticed it didn't grate on me half as badly as it had when I worked for him.

"Max, there was a man, maybe fifteen years ago. The agency used him to examine a series of near perfect passports."

"You have a good memory," he replied.

"Is he still alive?"

"The name you're searching for is Alonzo Galbraith."

"Alonzo Galbraith." I wrote the name on a note pad.

"Strange you should mention him. I just used him last month on another project. On most days, he divides his working time between our brothers at the FBI and the Library of Congress. He's at the Library most mornings but probably doesn't get there before ten o'clock. At heart these geniuses are lazy people."

"A new Durgan theory?" I asked.

"It keeps me from being jealous. Why do you want Alonzo?"

"I have an historical document I'd like authenticated and I need the best person I can find to do it," I answered.

Durgan gave me Galbraith's telephone number. "From what I hear, he loves to moonlight," Durgan added. "Loves the extra money."

If I had been right about Jefferson being an advanced CIA hologram, I was already the world-wide butt of a very sick joke. Caution made me give my office a thorough inspection before I called, looking for tiny monitors, anything suspicious, but I didn't know what to look for or how far hologram technology had advanced. Maybe they could produce holograms from a remote with no visible equipment. Still, I didn't see anything even vaguely suspicious.

After Durgan, I tried unsuccessfully to reach Alida at home. Then I called the hospital. This time the nurse's station connected me without question.

"No change," Alida said. "I don't like it, Brad. Twice last night the monitor in her room went flat and a team of nurses ran in with those electric-shock plates and got her heart started again. Between this and having to talk to Philip Norge, I'm a mess."

"Philip Norge?"

"He had me down at the police station for eight hours on Saturday and repeated the routine on Sunday."

"What did he want?"

"God only knows! But it got intense enough I insisted on my attorney being present."

I wondered what was in Norge's mind.

"Norge is a tin-badged sheriff. He's not my concern. Abbe is." Her voice faltered. She stopped to compose herself. "Abbe has a severe concussion. They think her brain is swollen. The doctor I spoke with doesn't offer hope."

"Alida, I'm sorry." I could hear sounds of her fighting back tears. The remark about a concussion sunk through the dense outer layer of my brain. "Concussion? I thought Abbe had passed out from the smoke!"

"No. Her doctors say she was struck hard on the back of her head."

"How?"

"Their guess is with a proverbial blunt instrument. Mine is Peter was wielding it. I wouldn't be surprised if he started the fire himself to cover his foul deed."

"Bruce told me they found a body in the ashes."

"If there's any justice in the world, the body will turn out to be Peter Mosley's."

"Maybe we'll know more when Abbe regains consciousness?" I suggested.

"If." Alida Pendragon, the realist, was preparing herself for the worse.

"Alida, she's getting the best medical care in the area," I said.

"I know." Alida sighed into the phone. "But sometimes I just don't think Abbe is going to survive this."

"Another premonition?"

"Maybe. There was something ominous in the way she pronounced the word.

"There could be more to Abbe Mosley and her will to survive than you give her credit for."

Alida didn't speak.

"Well, she's still alive! You wouldn't have thought it was possible four days ago!"

By the end of the conversation either I had boosted her spirits or she was kind enough to allow me to think I had.

"I appreciate your concern, Brad," she said.

"I'll be glad to come over and...."

"No. You have Kate. I'll be okay." There was a long pause. "And Brad! Thank you."

"Keep in touch. I'm here at the bookshop if you need me."

* * * * *

The mail was delivered just after we opened at ten. The invitation to the Christian Historical Trust's Halloween party sat on top. I lingered over the invitation. There was something about a "Christian" Halloween party—pagan ghosts mixed with saints and resurrection....

But there was no time to ponder this oxymoron. Two policemen knocked at my office door.

"Captain Norge wants to see you," one of them said.

"Can't this wait? I'm busy."

"Now!" the other one said, cutting off all further conversation.

I could have put up a fight, but in the end I would have gotten everybody angry, including myself. So I took Gordon off my lap and followed the cops downstairs. Gordon was not happy. He was probably already thinking of how to repay me for this slight.

Norge kept me waiting a half hour. He had me closeted in a small, fluorescent lit room which was decorated with a grey metal table and three cheap plastic and chrome chairs. With all this waiting, I would have thought I was back in the hospital, except there was no eight-year-old boy sticking his head around a corner, and I couldn't leave.

Norge arrived. He slammed a manila file folder down on the table and sat opposite me. He pushed the "record" button on a tape recorder which lay on the table between us and spoke both our names, the date, time, and location, all with crisp clarity. Finally, he began his questions—no preliminary niceties here.

"Where were you this weekend?"

"At the Outer Banks," I replied.

"Did you know I wanted to see you?"

"Yes."

"You don't take your civic responsibility seriously, do you?"

"Look! A close friend is going to have an operation and her

doctor suggested we get away together, which took precedent over talking with you."

"Over your legal obligations?"

"Norge, did you issue a warrant?"

Norge plowed ahead. "A body was found in Mosley's house."

"My bookshop manager told me."

"Did he also tell you we are now conducting a murder investigation?"

"No," I answered. "Who was killed?"

"Where were you early Thursday evening?"

"Am I a suspect?"

Norge gave me his tough, East L.A. glare. "We have a working theory the corpse is Mr. Peter Mosley. Mr. Mosley had filed a lawsuit against you," Norge said coldly. "Shortly thereafter, he reportedly threatened you. You draw your own conclusions!"

My mouth inadvertently opened.

"You still didn't answer my question? Where were you earlier on Thursday evening?"

"First, if I'm a suspect, I have the right to an attorney. You should have told me."

Norge cleared his throat to say something, but I cut him off.

"It's okay, I'll waive my right." I took a deep breath and continued. "I was at my bookshop, working." I was still cooperating but I didn't know for how long and I didn't like the way this conversation was turning.

"Can anyone verify it?"

I half-heartedly thought of telling Norge about Thomas Jefferson, but didn't. "No," I finally said.

"You hesitated."

"I was thinking back, wondering if I saw anyone on the street I knew."

"And you can't think of anyone," Norge clarified.

I thought about Jefferson again. "Correct," I said.

"What brought you to the Mosley house?"

I explained about Alida's phone call to Kate. "Abbe Mosley was leaving her husband. She had been staying at Alida Pendragon's house for a few days. Abbe went home to pick up some clothes around four, and when she didn't return by eight, Alida got worried and called Kate. She told Kate she was going out to check the Mosley house, and Kate promised we would meet her there."

"And Miss Pendragon was at Mosley's when you arrived?"

"With cellular telephone in hand. She had just called the fire department."

"Had she just arrived?"

"I assume so, but you'd have to ask her."

Norge straightened some of the papers in his file folder by tapping them against the desk top next to the recorder. The stenographer who would eventually transcribe the tape was going to love him. "I already did!" Norge said.

"And what did she say?"

Norge changed the subject again. "How did you get into the house?" Norge asked.

"Through the front door."

"Was it unlocked?"

"It was standing wide-open," I said.

My last remark seemed to surprise Norge. "And why did you look for Mrs. Mosley on the second floor?"

"Alida said Abbe went to the house for clothes and her bedroom was on the second floor."

"Miss Pendragon told me she had a "premonition"—the very word she used," Norge said.

"It happens."

"Did you have the same premonition?" Norge asked.

"No. As far as I'm concerned, I was lucky to find her at all. I didn't know where I was going. I shouldn't have rushed into the house in the first place."

Norge allowed a smirk to appear on his face. Obviously, this was his conclusion too. "When you found her, was there a beam or a wall on top of her?"

"No. She was lying quite still, alone, in the middle of the floor."

"Was there anything near her she could have hit her head on?"

I recreated the scene in my mind. "No furniture close enough," I said. "Alida has a theory Peter Mosley might have struck his wife before the fire started."

"Really?"

"Alida thinks he might have started the fire to cover up his attack. If your corpse is Peter, then something must have gone wrong and he ended up killing himself."

Norge considered this. "She's right!" he said. "If it is Mosley, something did go wrong, but he didn't kill himself."

I had no idea where Norge was going. "How can you be so sure?"

"The one thing we do know is the victim was dead before the fire started—from a bullet going in one side of his skull and out the other."

Now I was the one who was surprised. I sat quietly for a minute absorbing Norge's information, conscious of the tape recorder whirring on the table. "Could he have shot himself?" I asked.

"No weapon at the murder site," Norge said.

We were both silent again for almost a minute, the recorder providing white background sound. Finally Norge asked, "On the theory the corpse is Mosley, do you have any idea who might have killed him? Or why?"

"Most people I know didn't like Peter, but I can't think of anyone who would murder him."

Norge thought. "Well, it's just a theory for now. We haven't identified the corpse. It's charred beyond recognition, and we can't locate any dental records for Mosley."

There was silence again.

"What do you know about Miss Alida Pendragon?" Norge asked.

"Alida?"

"Alida! Miss Pengragon disliked Mosley because he beat his wife—motive. Miss Pendragon could have been at the Mosley's house earlier, found Mrs. Mosley unconscious, killed Mr. Mosley, and started the fire, herself—all before she called 911 and Miss Whitney from her portable cell phone—opportunity."

"If she did, why would she risk Abbe's life, leaving her in the burning house?"

Philip Norge didn't have an answer.

We sat through another long silence, which gave me a chance to think.

"When Abbe Mosley sold me the letter, she said there were more Jefferson letters where she found this one. I asked her how many, and she held out her fingers indicating a stack of letters four inches thick."

"How much would they be worth?"

I noted Norge's interest in the monetary value of things. "Fifty to a hundred real Jefferson letters? All unrecorded? A half million? A million dollars? It all depends on content."

"A million dollars is reason enough for murder," Norge concluded.

While we sat through another short silence, I thought back to something Alida had said. "Peter Mosley discovered Abbe's letter was missing because he had been checking the letters against his inventory. He told Abbe he was trying to sell them to a New York collector."

"Do you know who?" Norge asked.

"No. But there are always telephone records."

Norge took out his gold pen and spiral notebook. "I'll check. Maybe we'll catch a break and find a missing person on the other end."

Norge turned off the tape recorder and told me to call him

before leaving town. It was a line from a nineteen forties, grade "B" movie. He followed by asking if I would come out to the Mosley house with him later in the afternoon.

"Why?"

"See if you can find the letters, or what remains of them."

From suspect to assistant from one minute to the next; the same whipsaw effect I was feeling with Kate. I didn't trust Norge and I was beginning not to like him, but in the end, curiosity overcame my doubts and I promised I'd be there.

* * * * *

It was quarter of twelve before I got back to Parker's Rare Books. I hurriedly dialed the number Max Durgan had given me.

"Galbraith," a gravelly baritone said in a tone screaming, "Go Away!" I introduced myself and told Galbraith about meeting him years ago when I was with the CIA. "I'm an antiquarian bookseller now," I added.

"Life takes peculiar twists," Galbraith observed with total disinterest. "Now tell me what you want?"

"I want you to examine a letter supposedly written by Thomas Jefferson."

"You think it's a fake?"

"If it is, it's a good one. Keith Stanley appraised it and told me it was genuine."

"Keith Stanley's a whore!" Galbraith bellowed.

I pressed on. "Will you take a look at my letter? It's very important I learn the truth about it."

"Why? Is it life or death?" Galbraith laughed.

"I'm afraid it might be."

He suddenly became serious. "I charge one hundred and fifty dollars an hour, three hours minimum, payment in advance. I only take cash, no checks. I don't give written receipts or reports."

"Fair enough," I said, adding, "I need this done yesterday."

"Doesn't everybody?" Galbraith sighed. "Bring me the letter

tomorrow morning. Seven-thirty. The Library of Congress."

"Seven-thirty? I'll be coming from Williamsburg."

"Tomorrow morning, seven-thirty. It's then, or in three weeks. Take your pick. I'm a busy man."

I reluctantly agreed to seven-thirty. Galbraith told me how to enter the Library. He said he would leave my name with the guard. "He'll give you directions to my office."

"Okay."

"And remember," Galbraith added. "Bring cash! The letter alone isn't going to do you much good." I heard a click. Our conversation had ended with the receiver still at my ear. Tomorrow promised to be a humdinger.

Chapter Twelve

Long shadows streaked across the Mosley property late that afternoon. The house and the grounds were encircled with yellow police tape, as if the house itself was being quarantined for having an insidious disease. In a sense it was true, because murder is a sickness, and murder had been committed here.

I followed Philip Norge under the yellow tape and up the Mosley's front lawn. The tan paint on the house's wide-board siding was blistered and peeling. Inside the entry-way, a heavy layer of black soot clung to every surface. The office, where Peter Mosley had conducted his business and might have died, was missing an eight foot square of ceiling where the roof had collapsed. The fire department had covered the hole with a bright blue tarp. The fire had been at its hottest in Peter's office and the bookshelves lining the walls had been charred. All the books on them were destroyed. Those not totally burnt in the blaze were ruined by the firemen and their hoses. The room smelt of burnt wood and something else.

"Gasoline?" I asked.

"Twenty-four hours later and the smell's still overpowering, isn't it? Whoever did this generously poured it on everything, including the corpse. If the perpetrator was trying to make this look accidental, he or she failed miserably."

It might have been my imagination but I felt Norge had put an emphasis on the words "or she," a thinly veiled reference to Alida

Pendragon.

"Whoever did this was strictly an amateur," Norge continued.

"Maybe they just wanted you to think so."

Norge considered this. "By the way, I did check Mosley's phone records."

"And?"

"Does the name Anthony Calvado mean anything to you?"

"Yes! He's a prominent collector of Americana. He's got good taste and deep pockets."

"He's also heavily linked to organized crime," Norge said.

"Who told you that?"

"The F.B.I. They're not sure exactly where Calvado fits into the criminal food chain, but their guess is somewhere very close to the top." Norge paused. "Does he buy books from you?"

"Sometimes, if I can find anything interesting enough to tempt him. He's turned into a very sophisticated collector."

"From the number of telephone calls back and forth between Calvado and Mosley, I'd say the letters Mr. Mosley had were of *great* interest to him," Norge said.

"I found something very interesting, too, Philip," a voice said from around a corner.

Norge took two steps toward the voice and introduced me to Derrick Walters, a trim, fortyish black man who wore a name tag with the word "Captain" on it. Walters was in charge of arson investigation for the fire department.

"Look here," Walters said, lifting a remnant of the charred oriental rug, its rich design still visible through the soot. Underneath the rug was a metal track. "That's what got me curious," Walters said. The track led under a tall bookcase rising to the ceiling. "Then I found this catch on the far side of the bookcase holding it in place." Walters put his hand between the shelving and wall and I heard a click. "I opened it, gave the bookcase a push, and voilà."

The bookcase moved smoothly along the track revealing an

eight by ten foot room behind it. Surprisingly, the room was virtually untouched by the fire. There were two tables that ran ten feet from the opening to the far end. Over one of the tables was a hood you would normally find above a kitchen stove. It had its own light and exhaust fan for venting fumes. The entire room was a compact and very efficient bookbindery. There was a sewing frame, bookpress, microwave oven, rows of binder's rules and dingbats, large trays underneath the hood for washing prints or maps, an ultra-violet light with a magnifying glass in the center, a small guillotine paper-cutter, and a series of pigeon-hole compartments under the table to hold supplies. Mosley stocked a large number of papers for matching hurt copies of books, and a wide assortment of leathers.

"Jesus," Norge said. "I should have found this earlier!" He acted as if he had accidentally kicked a corpse.

"The cinder-block walls protected it from the fire," Walters observed.

I walked into the room. On the right was a small bookcase with four shelves. I picked up one of the books and opened the front cover. Inside was an uncanceled bookplate from the Library of Congress. I went down the row. All of the volumes had library markings. I couldn't be certain without checking, but I would have bet a considerable amount of money they were stolen. There was a Vesalius, a Smith's *Virginia*—a true first with the four folding maps in fine condition—another tract on Virginia dated 1608, and a lovely eighteenth century flower book by Edwards I had never seen before. It had at least a hundred exquisite, hand-colored plates. The books were on varying subjects but they were all very expensive. Most probably they didn't belong to Peter Mosley.

I showed Norge the bookplates. "It's standard practice for libraries to stamp 'Withdrawn' on books they actually deaccession."

"Deaccession?"

"Sell," I said.

"Libraries sell books?" This concept seemed to offend Norge.

"They get second and third copies of books and others outside their collecting interests. It's a good way to redistribute the wealth," I said, and added, "Take these to a safe place! There's a half-million dollars worth of books here."

I had Norge's full attention. He came into the room to see for himself what a half-million dollars worth of books looked like. When he did, I moved to the far end. On a small bookshelf there, I picked up a magnificent copy of Newton's *Principia*, recently rebound in handsome dark brown leather. The copy was absolutely fine. There were no library stamps here, in fact no visible marks of any past ownership at all.

"This must have been Peter Mosley's book hospital," I said. "From what I'm seeing, Peter reconditioned stolen books by removing marks which could trace them back to their origins." I pointed. "I'll bet the ultra-violet lamp was used to find hidden codes."

"Codes?" Norge asked.

"Some libraries write on specific pages in ink you can only see under ultra-violet light. Helps prove the books are theirs."

Norge's eyes were still on the half million dollars. He didn't hear what I was saying.

"It must have been quite a business: steal a book, make it untraceable, and sell it for pure profit."

While Norge's attention was on the books in front of him, I examined the bins of older paper underneath the counter. Bookbinders use these sheets to repair older books. With the right paper a good binder can make a repair virtually invisible. My eyes stopped on a ten inch stack of white paper near the far end of the room. I reached down and picked up a sheet, rubbed it between my fingers, then held it to the light. There was a watermark, but I couldn't place it with certainty.

Norge was still thumbing through the library books with his back towards me. I folded the sheet of paper and slipped it into my inside jacket pocket. I thought of asking Norge's permission, but I didn't know what his answer might be, and I didn't want to arouse his curiosity. Not yet!

When Norge finished, he said, "Jesus Christ! Don't they have security in these libraries?"

"Librarians do what they can."

"Well, they ought to get their act together." It was his final observation about the world of books, a world I'm sure he wished never to see again.

Norge was disappointed I couldn't find traces of the missing letters. Between us we searched Mosley's entire book hospital shelf by shelf. No success.

When we got outside, standing next to my car, Norge asked, "When are you going to get the Jefferson letter back?"

"Keith Stanley mailed it, but the Postal Service can't find it," I said.

"I know," Norge said. "It was sent registered mail, return receipt requested."

"That's what he told me."

"Me, too," Norge said.

I stood silently waiting for Norge to make his point. The whipsaw effect, from suspect to colleague to suspect again, was getting old.

Norge cleared his throat. "When they do find it, the Postal Service will deliver it to me. I'll hold it as evidence."

I think Norge was expecting an argument, instead I smiled and said, "Okay."

Norge started walking away.

"One last thing. Has it occurred to you what the odds are on having two large collections of unrecorded Jefferson letters turn up a few years apart in Williamsburg, Virginia?"

"Two?" Norge asked.

"The Christian Historical Trust owns one set, and then there's

Mosley's." I had piqued Norge's interest and I didn't even mention money.

"Go on."

"Nobody else has found a group of Jefferson letters this large in over a hundred years. Now two pop up."

"So?"

"You've got to consider the two collections might only be one."

"I already have," Norge said, smiling. "I talked with Theodore Jay over the weekend and asked him if any of his Jefferson letters were missing. We both went over to the Taliaferro-Cole house and checked. They were all there."

"How would you know if what you saw were real Jefferson letters?" I asked.

"I wouldn't." Norge beamed. "That's why I brought along John Harding from Swem Library at the College. He verified they were."

"Did you ask Jay if Mosley ever borrowed them?"

"I did, and Jay swore, except for Parke Hollingshed, no one else had even seen them."

"Would Jay know if Hollingshed had taken them to Mosley?"

"I asked Jay that same question. He told me I was crazy." Norge had a satisfied grin on his face. "I know you think I'm a dumb cop, but I've been at this investigating business for a long time."

"I see you've thought of everything," I said. Norge didn't hear the irony in my voice, or didn't let me know he had. We shook hands. As I drove away, my thoughts were already on tomorrow morning and my meeting with Alonzo Galbraith. I hoped I was doing the right thing. I had a disturbing pattern of rushing into situations I shouldn't. What would be the results next time?

* * * * *

Kate had telephoned the bookshop when I was out. I finally reached her at Chez Bayou.

"Alida called," Kate began. "Things are not going well for Abbe.

Alida asked me if I would stay over at her house tonight. She thinks Abbe is very close to death and she doesn't want to spend the night alone."

"You don't need my permission."

"I know, but I wanted to ask anyway."

I casually mentioned going to Washington early the next morning. I said I would be back by noon.

"That's when I have to start my purge for the operation," Kate reminded me.

The thought of drinking vile liquid made me gag. There was something about it which reminded me of Socrates.

Kate and I talked for another five minutes. When we finished, I asked, "Is Napoleon there?" I didn't explain why I wanted Napoleon, and to her credit, Kate didn't ask.

Thirty seconds later I heard Napoleon's voice. "Yo!"

"Remember the package I asked you to keep for me?"

"Uh huh."

"I need it."

"You going to be at the bookshop later tonight?" Napoleon asked.

"Yes."

"Bring it by around nine. Good for you?"

"It's perfect. Ask Kate for the key. I'll leave the alarm system off."

* * * * *

I sat in my office. My anxiety had grown to the point where work became impossible. I reached into my bottom drawer, took out a half-empty bottle of Dewar's scotch, and poured myself a double shot, neat. I sat there sipping it, knowing Jefferson would come, and he didn't disappoint. I looked at the wall clock. It was eight-thirty. Jefferson stood again in the doorway.

"You're not going to get upset this time, are you?" Jefferson asked.

I heard myself saying, "No! Why don't you have a seat?"

"Thank you," Jefferson answered, and did just that. He sat leaning forward on the edge of my three-cushion, red-leather Chesterfield couch. He wore a short jacket, a vest, and a white linen shirt. His trousers reminded me of knickers, with the bottom of his cuffs tied over his white, knee-length socks. His shoes were black with silver buckles. They seemed loose fitting. "I must get some help," he said. "I need to have a group of inflammatory letters destroyed, letters some people actually think I wrote."

"And what letters are they?" I heard myself asking. I knew I had just crossed over some imaginary line. Before, when I talked to Jefferson, I hadn't suspected he was a hallucination, but now I did, and I was having a conversation with him anyway. According to the medical books, the next stage would begin with Jefferson suggesting I enter his world and do something to help him. It was all following a predictable script. I would gradually serve his needs and everything would reverse—my real world would become a dream, and Jefferson's world, my reality.

"These are letters I was supposed to have written to my friend, John Adams," Jefferson was explaining. There were too many thoughts buzzing through my mind to concentrate fully on what he was saying.

I had to remember to tell my psychiatrist, when one was assigned, about the real letter Abbe Mosley had offered me, a letter also written to John Adams. Someday I might laugh about how my subconscious mind introduced a real event into this concoction.

"And what did the letters say?" I asked.

"That when I was President, I proposed a plot to hand the country back to England."

I really didn't know from what part of my brain that thought had come, but I was certain, with therapy, I could eventually tell. Everything we think and do is connected.

It wasn't surprising I thought thoughts of the eighteenth century, living in Williamsburg as I did, and Thomas Jefferson was the most logical person for my mind to conjure up. I was grateful I didn't live in Orlando, Florida. Had I, no doubt I might have been conversing with a round, decidedly upbeat, talking mouse.

"So you understand the gravity of the situation?" Jefferson asked, bringing my attention back to the matter at hand.

I didn't answer. At this point, I was walking around Jefferson looking intently for signs I might be speaking with an interactive hologram. I was looking, unsuccessfully, for the technical equivalent of strings on a puppet. "Where did you see the letters?" I asked.

"The Coke-Garrett House."

I looked confused.

"At the large white house on Nicholson Street."

"The President's house?"

"I've also heard people refer to it as that. I read the letters while the owner of the house, a plain sort of man,..."

"*Very* plain," I cut in.

Jefferson smiled. I was glad to see my hallucination/hologram had a sense of humor. "This 'plain' man had dinner with another. They were discussing the letters. His friend—thin, with short grey hair and reading spectacles—he was the one writing a book about the letters, a book would brand me a traitor to my country."

"That would be Parke Hollingshed," I said. As I did, I walked behind Jefferson and waved my hand over his head. His image remained unaffected.

"The letters look very much like my handwriting," Jefferson continued. "They are most detailed. The lies are woven with true facts about my life. They were written from places where I actually was, on the dates when I abided there. Many of the chatty asides are remarks I did make, both publicly and in private. If I didn't know the letters to be outrageous lies, I myself would have difficulty denying them. This is a diabolical plot, sir. Something worthy of Mr. Hamilton." Jefferson leaned forward and added in a conspiratorial whisper, "At heart, he was a monarchist, you know."

I was back sitting at my desk when I heard the buzzer sound downstairs. Someone had opened the door. "Napoleon, I'm upstairs!" I hollered. I looked down at my drink. My glass was empty; I put it back in the drawer.

I heard Napoleon climb the steps two at a time. He looked at me and then over at the leather couch on which my hologram/hallucination sat.

"Yo!" he said, then turned to me. "Brad, here's your envelope." He looked in Jefferson's direction. "Sorry, didn't know you had a visitor."

"A visitor?" I repeated.

"The red-headed dude in the costume."

I had an instant moment of relief, complete and reassuring, then I feared I might have imagined, or somehow misunderstood, what Napoleon had said, so I asked, "The man sitting on the couch?"

"Yeah." Napoleon looked over at Jefferson. "Napoleon Jones," he said, introducing himself.

"Thomas Jefferson," my hallucination/hologram replied.

"Like the President!"

Gordon came into the room and seeing Jefferson sitting on the couch, made a short leap to claim his lap. He went right through Jefferson's legs and landed hard against the side of the couch.

"Not 'like the President,'" I explained to Napoleon. "He *is* the President." Whatever Jefferson really was, he was no longer *my* hallucination alone.

"You mean I'm talking to a ghost?" Napoleon said.

"I prefer the term 'spectral image,'" Jefferson answered.

While he was speaking, Gordon sprang to his feet and shook himself, as if he had fallen into water. Then, he lifted his tail perpendicular and walked out of the room, as if to say, "I meant to do that!"

Napoleon had been more prepared to accept Jefferson as a ghost than I. For me, the transition between Jefferson, the hallucination, and Jefferson, the ghost—or "spectral image"—took longer. My initial sense of relief over not having a hallucination only I could see was quickly replaced by a feeling of emotional vertigo. For me, ghosts were a spiritual presence confined to myth and legend. The visual existence of this spirit challenged my entire belief system. Yet, I couldn't find any sign Thomas Jefferson was a hologram. My only hope with a rational, scientific theory, was that technology had completely outstripped my ability to detect it. I couldn't explain what Jefferson was or why he became visible to Napoleon and me, not to mention Gordon.

"Well, my grand-mama, she believed in ghosts," Napoleon reassured me. "Made money off them too, chasin' them out of neighbor houses, putting gris-gris on them." He sat in the chair opposite the desk.

Jefferson remained on the couch. "No one else can see me except for the two of you and the cat," Jefferson tried to explain, "I'm not certain why, but I hypothesize both of you have been ordained to help me with my problem."

"Ordained? Ordained by who?" Napoleon asked.

"Whom!" Jefferson posed like Rodin's Thinker. "I don't know by whom," Jefferson finally answered. "God, perhaps?"

"Didn't think you believed in God."

"But I do, citizen. I always have. What I never believed in was the Church, which I perceived as an institution of Man, whose purpose was to amass personal wealth and power for a priestly class." Jefferson paused. "Several times in the hundred and seventy odd years since my body died, I've thought I could have been placed here as a spectral image as punishment for my disbelief in the institution. Logically, I know it to be absurd, but I've been searching for a reason to explain my current predicament."

"Maybe life is preordained?" I suggested. "Maybe you are a spirit because you have unfinished business?"

"Because of the letters? Am I here in Williamsburg to save my reputation?" he asked in hope.

"What letters you talkin' about?" Napoleon asked.

Both Jefferson and I told Napoleon about the letters.

"How come you don't just take them?" Napoleon asked Jefferson.

"In my present state I cannot affect physical objects." Jefferson stood. "Observe. I can pick up a book to read it and an image of the book is in my hands, but the real, physical book remains where it was." Jefferson demonstrated. "I can open my version of the book, page through it, even mark passages with my own pen, but the real book stays on the shelf. If I return my version of the book, your physical book remains untouched and unmarked. My version will cease to be."

"What if you leave the book out, on the table?" Napoleon asked.

"It will vanish when I am through with it."

"A damn neat world you live in!" Napoleon said.

Jefferson smiled. "It certainly is not without its advantages, sir. It's ironic. During my life, I was fastidiously neat in order to be more efficient, in order not to waste time. Since I died I have experienced time enough for four lives—more, since I exist without sleep. I have time to squander, and the things keeping me from my books—sleep, disarray—now, they all are taken care of for me."

Part of me was beginning to enjoy Jefferson's rambling, the thoughts of a great man from another time, but out of the corner of my eye, I could see Napoleon shifting in his chair.

"Where are the letters now?" Napoleon asked, bringing Jefferson back to the present.

Jefferson's eyes widened. He seemed to be on the edge between concern and panic. "I don't know."

"You want us to steal letters for you and you don't know where they are? You better find out! Ain't going to go thievin' through every house in Williamsburg looking for them."

Jefferson stood, hands on hips. "I don't like your attitude, sir!" he said emphatically.

"Don't like no nigger talking down to you, is what you mean!" Jefferson's eyes blazed.

"I heard about you," Napoleon continued. "You owned slaves. You even had your way with one of them."

"You judge me by the sensitivity of your own time, sir," Jefferson said. "But when I lived, I was in my time, not yours, and I lived by the rules of the society surrounding me."

"You may have done what you wanted in the past," Napoleon answered. "But now you in *my* time. You want me to do some thievin', you better start showing some respect."

The conversation was developing an edge. I interrupted. "I have a pretty good idea where the letters might be." They both stopped arguing and looked in my direction. "The police captain, Philip Norge, told me he had just seen the letters this past Sunday at the Taliaferro-Cole house, in some sort of vault. Look for the letters there."

"They might have taken them someplace else by now," Napoleon said.

"Maybe but Hollingshed and Jay have the Trust's board meeting coming up. They'll want the letters at hand for show and tell."

"How can we be certain?" Jefferson asked.

"We can't. One of us has got to search the house for them," I answered. Both Napoleon and I looked at Jefferson. "And since one of us has certain unique attributes...."

"Like nobody can see him."

"I think he should be our sleuth," I said.

Jefferson looked from Napoleon to me and back again. "Very well."

"Back here tomorrow evening at eight-thirty then?" I asked, not believing the words came from my mouth.

"At the bookstore," Napoleon said.

"I feel relieved, gentlemen. At last we have a plan,"

I didn't share Jefferson's confidence. I don't think Napoleon did either.

* * * * *

I called the hospital before I went to sleep and asked for Alida. Kate came to the phone. "Abbe Mosley just died," Kate said. "I'm sorry."

I could hear Alida's sobbing in the background. "It's okay," Kate finally said. "There was a great deal of brain damage. It wouldn't have been much of a life for her if she had lived."

"Doesn't change the sorrow we all feel, does it?"

"No, but it makes it more bearable," Kate replied.

"Should I come over there?"

"No, babe, Alida and I are fine together. Really, there's nothing you can do. I think we both would appreciate being by ourselves tonight, just us girls."

Chapter Thirteen

୰ଌ

On Tuesday morning, I walked into the Library of Congress through the back door, off the courtyard on Second Street. It was the entrance the Library employees use, although there weren't many of them coming to work at seven-fifteen. I gave my name to the guard and he found it on a list attached to his clipboard.

"The elevator's broken to Galbraith's wing," the guard warned, handing me a plastic visitor's badge.

"Are there stairs?" I asked.

"Down the corridor." The guard pointed. "First door on your left. Then all the way up. Five flights." He said it as if he were describing the way to Mount Everest.

"You get lost, go to a phone. We'll come find you."

I took a step in the direction he was pointing. "Hold it!" the guard said loudly. "What's in the envelope?"

"A letter for Mr. Galbraith to see."

"You want to bring it out with you, have Galbraith sign a release form. He forgets sometimes. Absent-minded professor."

I nodded and began walking down a long concrete ramp with steel I-beams overhead. There were no magnificent tile mosaics here in the Library of Congress' working area, the rooms the public rarely sees. I found the door the guard had mentioned and began climbing the stairs. My noise echoed. I began feeling claustrophobic. I realized I was in the bowels of the Library of Congress,

America's largest and arguably most prestigious library, and all I found were employees' quarters with the grace and charm of a maximum security prison.

The five flights of stairs turned out to be ten, with two levels of stacks comprising one floor. When I got to the top, I stopped to wipe the sweat off my face. I was breathing heavily. I needed to get back to the gym.

The fifth floor was the same as the others I had seen on my walk up, with grey concrete corridors, matching metal doors, cinder block walls, and fluorescent lights. I walked down the hall until I came to a door with the word "Galbraith" painted in a white, arcane stencil. I tried the knob, which was locked. Then I rapped loudly on the door with the palm of my hand.

It was opened by a tall, trim man who appeared to be in his early forties. "You're on time," he said. "It's a good start." Then he paused. "You are Parker, aren't you?" He spoke rapidly, in short bursts, like a machine gun.

"And you must be Galbraith."

"You bring the letter?" Galbraith asked.

I handed him the envelope.

"How about the money?"

I took out four hundred and fifty dollars from my inside jacket pocket and offered it to him.

He shook his head. "No! Not allowed to accept money." He pointed to his desk in the corner of the ante-room where we were standing. "Look at my copy of *A Link Between the Days*. It's a new book by Dennis Montgomery. When you finish why don't you join me in the laboratory."

I must have looked confused.

"Some people forget and leave money in the book," Galbraith explained. "I don't know who. So I just hold it for a while. Maybe someone will come back, I tell myself, but they never do."

I put my four hundred and fifty dollars inside the rear cover and followed Galbraith to the next room. It was a gigantic, slightly curved laboratory, carved out of at least three office suites. It had considerable counter space and a large assortment of microscopes, enclosed chambers, and electronic instruments I don't have names for. The most impressive element of the room was an uninterrupted picture window running the entire length of the far wall, from waist level to ceiling. The window reminded me of the ones in large, luxury boxes corporations rent for professional football games. I walked over to it.

"My God!" I said. "This is remarkable!" Galbraith's laboratory was just under the Library of Congress's main dome. Above us was the dirt encrusted dome itself, far below the library's main reading room, with tables, chairs, and desks arranged, from our vantage point, in a wondrous mosaic.

"I wish I could tell you I got used to it, working here day after day," Galbraith said, looking out the window with me, "but I haven't. When I do stop to look, it still takes my breath away, just like it did the first time." Galbraith was holding the Jefferson letter now, his attention switched to it, his hands tenderly caressing the paper. It was a sensual experience watching him work. "Now, tell me what you know about this letter."

I did. I told him about how Abbe Mosley had brought the letter to me, and who her husband was. I thought the name "Peter Mosley" brought a slight twitch to Galbraith's left eyelid. I could have imagined it. Who knows? In any event, Galbraith didn't stop me to comment on Mosley and I didn't ask. Then, I told Galbraith of sending the letter to Keith Stanley.

"Stanley!" Galbraith sputtered derisively. "Keith Stanley sells people faith. Faith George Washington actually signed a letter! Faith Winston Churchill wrote his name in a copy of one of his books! Unless it's an obvious forgery, there's no way to prove it's genuine, not just from a signature. You sign a piece of paper, your signature's different if you're standing or sitting, relaxed or in an emotional state. Now, Stanley will swear the letter he's selling you is real, but in many cases he has no proof.

"What I do is science. I spent the last fifteen years of my life working with the finest equipment the F.B.I. could offer and I was trained by the best forensic experts in the country, which is the difference between Stanley and me."

"It's why I'm here," I said. "I want 'real proof.'"

"Then go out, get some breakfast and give me two hours with this letter of yours. I'll have results by then."

I thought about the ten flights of steps. Maybe the elevator would be fixed by the time I returned.

* * * * *

I called Alida's house from a drug store on Constitution Avenue. Kate answered. "How are things?" I asked.

"Alida and I sat up most of the night talking. She's asleep now."

"How is she doing?"

"She's sad, but I wouldn't worry about her. Alida Pendragon is a very strong woman. She knows how to deal with loss."

"When do you start your purge?" I asked.

"Don't remind me! Noon."

"I should be back in Williamsburg around one," I said.

"Well don't rush home on my account unless you get some sort of thrill watching a girl go to the bathroom."

"Voyeurism could be fun."

For some reason Kate laughed. "Only you! Well, drive safely."

* * * * *

Miracles do happen! When I returned to the Library of Congress two hours later, the elevator to the fifth floor was fixed. There were at least six other people working in the lab then. Galbraith herded me into a small conference room at the far end, and shut the door.

"Let me start with a little background," Galbraith began his lecture. "In a court of law there are four categories for authenticating a document: it is *most probably* genuine, it is *probably* genuine, it's *probably not* genuine, and it *most probably isn't* genuine. As a witness, I never say anything is a hundred percent fake or a hundred percent real."

"What about my letter?" I asked.

"From a legal standpoint, your letter is in a fifth category. Dead in the middle. I'd make a terrible witness with this one."

"We're not in court. I want your best educated assessment."

Galbraith hesitated for a moment. He looked out the window staring across the library's dome. "It's a fake!" he finally said. "A damned clever fake, but, in the end, a fake."

"Why?"

"I'm going to sound like Keith Stanley. 'Instinct!'" Galbraith looked at me and then at the letter I had given him. "Start with the handwriting. It looks like Jefferson's. It was written with a pen Jefferson might have used. Whoever wrote this letter—and for the sake of argument let's assume it's a forgery—is very good, must of spent hundreds of hours perfecting his technique. Even the wording is Jeffersonian, the style, construction, the grammar...." Galbraith waved his hand dismissively, before he continued. "If you have a suspect in mind, I'll wager he spent a lot of time with the big Jefferson collections. Check with Manuscripts here, they'll tell you who has been at the Jefferson documents and for how long. When do you think the forgery was made?"

"I'm not sure. Two to four years ago?"

"Too many sign-in sheets to page through," Galbraith said. "Pity!"

"What about the paper and ink?"

"The paper's very fine stationery, definitely eighteenth century, most probably French. There is a watermark. I can come up with a manufacturer's name if you really need it. I don't know if Jefferson bought this brand of paper when he was in Paris, but he could have. A little work with our Jefferson letters, I might find a match." Galbraith peered at me from over his half-glasses. "For an additional fee, of course."

"Of course," I replied. Whatever else he was, Max Durgan was right on target about people.

"I also tested a fleck of ink," Galbraith continued. "It's standard eighteenth century iron gaul ink. No modern impurities in the fleck I examined."

Galbraith paused. "Now, the paper's right, and the ink's right, but what disturbs me is the bond between them."

"What do you mean?"

"After almost two hundred years, the ink should have fused more with the paper."

I watched Galbraith, waiting for more of an explanation. Finally I said, "I guess I don't understand the significance."

"I think someone wrote this letter very recently and aged it artificially. Most forgers do this in a microwave oven. It's very exacting work. You leave the letters in the microwave too long, you get a cracking of the ink which is an obvious, tell-tale sign the letter was baked. Our forger didn't. But what I think our man did was to undercook this sucker by about five seconds. He was very close, and he erred on the right side by not overcooking. This letter is really a work of genius. You'd never notice the bond unless you were specifically looking for problems, and even then, the bond is good enough to pass a test for two-hundred-year-old documents. But instinct tells me, it's not right."

From my inside jacket pocket I removed a folded sheet of stationery, the one I had taken from Peter Mosley's bookbindery. I handed it to Galbraith.

"What's this?" he asked, feeling the paper as tenderly as he did before. He held it up to the light looking for a watermark.

"Is it the same stationery the Jefferson letter's written on?"

"Yes!" Galbraith said without hesitation. "Same watermark; same chain-lines. Where did you find this?"

"In a stack with at least five hundred sheets of blank paper just like it."

Galbraith sat back. "The odds on this letter being a forgery just went up," he mumbled almost to himself. "Too bad you don't have more letters for me to examine."

"What if I could find more?"

Galbraith's glance went from the paper to my face. He smiled. "Could you?"

"It's a possibility."

"If you could, I'd examine them for free!" Galbraith was not the type of man to say this lightly.

"How many letters would you need?"

Galbraith sat back in his chair. "Thirty? The chances of a forger writing a perfect letter like this one must be a thousand to one. If I had, say, thirty letters to examine, the possibility of all thirty being perfect—well, it couldn't happen."

"And what if they all turn out to be perfect?" I asked.

"Then we'll know the letters are real."

We sat in the conference room for the next half hour discussing how to proceed.

Chapter Fourteen

◈

Driving back from Washington I concluded I was more comfortable with Jefferson, the hallucination, than with Jefferson, the spectral image, or whatever he was. Part of my mind still held to the hologram theory, even though I hadn't been able to find any physical evidence to substantiate it. It had been easier for Napoleon to accept Jefferson as a ghost. After all, Napoleon's grandmother earned money exorcising spirits like Jefferson from people's homes. But in my cultural background, people did not believe in things which went bump in the night. We were all sober, rational, God-fearing, American Protestants, and seeing and consorting with ghosts wasn't part of our overall package.

My own religious view on what happens when we die is understandably vague. I simply never gave the matter much thought. Over the years, I came to accept the tenet: we humans all have souls, and this aspect of us, our best, remains a constant part of the Universe. Death merely returns our souls to God. The rest? Maybe it simply ended!

I had read somewhere Navajos believe a similar concept. With their belief, the true spirit of man returns to creation, but Navajos add a twist. In their version, man's bad and evil remain behind as "chindi," which causes sickness and grief.

Was the ghost of Jefferson his "chindi?" Did this spirit Napoleon and I both saw, represent all the bad and evil Jefferson did in his life? Would my life or Napoleon's be touched by it? Did Jefferson have unhealthy, unholy reasons for wanting us to destroy his letters? Or was this all a sick CIA joke?

The drive back from my meeting with Galbraith had released a torrent of questions. After Napoleon saw Jefferson, I had to accept Jefferson was a reality, but the question remained—what kind of a reality was he? If he were a ghost, I wanted to think he might be the remaining spirit of one of our founding fathers, rising up once again to meet a very real challenge, but I couldn't discount deeper, darker forces at work. Was Jefferson still the inspirational patriot, or was he the "evil" Christians pray God to "deliver us from?" And I still wasn't convinced he wasn't one of Max Durgan's nasty technological experiments?

Jefferson, the hallucination, was becoming the preferable concept. In fact, I was actually developing a nostalgia for him, the way some people do when remembering Richard Nixon. Being crazy was not a good thing, but my own insanity was somehow more comforting and manageable than dealing with the mysteries of the universe. Now I was face to face with a force I did not understand. I didn't like this situation at all.

* * * * *

I arrived at Alida's house at one.

"Kate went home to purge herself," Alida said as a greeting.

"How are *you* doing?"

"Sad, but fine. You have lunch yet?"

We ate at her dining room table. She served ham and cheese sandwiches, salad, and a glass of Cotes du Rhone. Outside, halfway between the house and the river, a deer with four-point antlers was munching on one of Alida's azalea bushes. Alida didn't seem to notice or care.

"I had hope until very near the end," Alida told me. "The last few hours were painful. Abbe thrashed in her bed. It was as if she were willing herself to wake up and talk to us, but she didn't have the strength."

"You were very good to Abbe, the few days before the accident."

"This was no accident, Brad," Alida said. "This was murder, and her husband, may he rest in hell, committed it."

"Maybe, but if the corpse turns out to be Peter, he was murdered too." I gave her Norge's report of the bullet hole in the skull.

"Then who killed Peter and Abbe? Do the police have a suspect?"

"Norge thinks it might be you." I had given her no warning; I wanted to see an honest reaction.

"*Me?*" Alida's face darkened and puffed. "So, the truth about all the weekend questioning comes out! Nobody actually accused me of anything, but I'm damned glad my lawyer was there. Damn! You know, if it turns out the body is Peter's, I really could have killed him." Alida was chomping on her sandwich and gesturing with her fork as she spoke. "Norge has a right to his suspicions, but he doesn't know me. I would have acted to keep Abbe safe from Peter, but I would have done it within the system. I never did believe in vigilantes."

Between bites of food, I asked Alida, "What did Abbe tell you about the letter?"

"Not terribly much. She mentioned she should have known better than to give it to you."

"I'm not so bad," I answered with mock hurt.

"This has nothing to do with you, Brad Parker, and you know it! Abbe could predict how Peter might react, but she went ahead anyway. She was more determined to get the money to leave than she was to protect herself."

"But what else did she tell you about the letters?"

"Abbe told both of us there was a stack of them."

"Probably a hundred or more by her description."

"Abbe said Peter had so many Jefferson letters, she didn't see how he could know one was missing."

"But he did," I replied.

"Bad luck! I told you about his matching the letters to his inventory sheets. She should have known, but with Peter's reputation, surviving the marriage meant not paying close attention to what Peter did."

"Abbe played ostrich?"

"Exactly! See no evil; evil does not exist. Anyway, Abbe told me she was surprised to find the Jefferson letters in the first place. She was sure Peter had sold them to the Trust years ago." Alida took a mouthful of lettuce. I looked out the window at the deer, still munching on the azalea plant.

"Maybe Jay consigned the letters back to Mosley."

"He could have. Parke Hollingshed probably was finished with them."

"Jay might have decided to sell them and recoup some of his costs."

"He denied it," I said.

"Denied? To whom?"

"Philip Norge." My mind was racing. "I wonder where Peter found the letters in the first place."

"Abbe didn't say."

"Funny, I never heard about any sale. You know what a small world the book business is."

"Well, it doesn't make any difference now," Alida said. "The letters must have burned in the fire."

I wondered, or were the letters in the Taliaferro-Cole House? Logic favored one collection. Theodore Jay might have been wrong about their never leaving the Trust. Who knows? He did seem anxious to buy Abbe's lone letter from me. All I had was idle speculation. I didn't *know* anything.

I stayed with Alida for another half hour. There were several moments when I almost told her about Alonzo Galbraith and

Jefferson, but at times discretion can be the better part of valor, even for me.

* * * * *

Kate gave me a warm hug and kiss when I got to her apartment. "What did I just taste?" she asked me.

"Alida gave me salad and a sandwich for lunch."

"I can only eat jello," Kate said mournfully.

"I'm sorry."

I heard Kate's stomach rumble. "Excuse me," she said and quickly ran into the bathroom.

"How was Washington?" she asked through the closed door.

"Good!"

"What were you doing there? I never asked."

"I wanted to find out if a manuscript I had was a forgery or not," I answered.

"Were you successful?"

"The results were inconclusive."

"In Washington they usually are," Kate said. "It's not a very good place to look for anything definitive."

I laughed.

I stayed with Kate in her apartment for two hours. Kate made ten additional quick dashes to the bathroom. Her medicine might have a repulsive taste, but it certainly did work.

I finally left for Parker's Rare Books just before four. I wanted to talk to Bruce about the next few days. I didn't know what was going to happen tomorrow with Kate, and I had to be certain the hours and assignments were covered at the bookshop, no matter what.

For the time being, I watched Kate yo-yo back and forth from living room to toilet. I wasn't much help.

"Go to the bookshop," she finally said.

"I will. See you about nine-thirty. If it's okay, I'll stay over."

"Good!" Kate replied. "We have an early start tomorrow."

*****

When I got to the bookshop, Norge was sitting on the low wall separating Parker's from Rustermann's Restaurant. If I hadn't known better, I would have thought he was a nattily dressed tourist.

"You keep banker's hours!" Norge said.

"How are your inquiries coming?" I asked.

"Well, Abbe Mosley's death makes this a murder investigation."

"No luck yet in finding out who belongs to the corpse in Peter's office?"

"Pardon the pun but it's a temporary dead-end," Norge replied, waving his hand in the air as if he were shooing a fly. "If Mosley's still alive, there are no reported sightings." Norge paused, as if expecting a reply. "And I sure haven't been able to find Mosley's dental records to prove one way or another the corpse is him, at least not with denists within a sixty mile radius. Your friend apparently never visited a dentist."

"If they exist, you'll find them."

Norge shrugged his shoulders. "No matter. Peter's wife is dead, it's an official murder investigation anyway. We're talking to the F.B.I. about extraditing Anthony Calvado to Williamsburg."

"You think he had anything to do with this?" I asked.

"Who knows? At least it'll rattle his cage. You've got to do this to the bad guys now and then." Norge stood up, pointed his index finger at me as if it were a gun, and walked away.

*****

When Bruce left the shop at six, he had four pages of a notepad filled with assignments and to-dos. From the overwhelmed look on his face, I was sure I wasn't going to be missed no matter how long I was away.

In my office, I sat thinking and sipping Dewar's. I didn't normally drink on a daily basis, but I justified this round with the lie: scotch was helping my mind process the meaning of Jefferson's life after death. Then, I heard sounds at the door downstairs. I looked at the clock. It was only seven-thirty.

"Yo!" Napoleon shouted. I could hear him locking the door behind him.

"You're early," I said.

"We got talkin' to do," Napoleon began. "Just the two of us. No ghosts allowed."

"About helping Jefferson?"

"Or not," Napoleon's eyes had an intensity I'd never seen in him before. "No way I gonna steal no letters for no ghost!"

"I've been thinking similar thoughts," I said softly.

Napoleon continued as if he didn't hear me. "Those letters are worth enough money to be grand theft. With my priors, grand theft means ten to thirty years depending on the judge. I did my service to the state already and I don't want to do no more."

"You ever stop and think the letters might be genuine?" It was a thought that had lurked in the deep recesses of my brain all day. Mr. Dewar had just brought the idea to the surface.

"You mean Jefferson's just trying to cover his own butt!"

"Exactly!"

"I know it's the kind of thing you white boys do," Napoleon reflected. "It's a possibility."

"And if we destroyed the letters, we would be destroying part of American history."

"Don't care about American history, but I do worry a lot about jail time and covering my own sorry ass. I can just see myself. 'Judge, have mercy! I didn't steal the letters for money. I stole them for a ghost. For American history!'"

I laughed.

"I'd spend half my prison time in a psycho ward. In a stir funny-farm, they shoot you up with drugs day after day 'til you *are* crazy, no matter how you started out. Then you stay crazy for the rest of your life. I seen it happen too often. No, sir! Not me!" Napoleon shook his head and began pacing.

119

"Maybe there's another way."

Napoleon stopped. "You have a plan?"

"Not yet."

"Good," Napoleon said. "All my life, I get in trouble listening to white folk got plans."

I found another glass in my drawer and poured three inches of scotch, neat, for Napoleon. We sat there, sipping in silence, until Napoleon asked me what I did in the C.I.A. I told him some things.

"What you like to do most?" he asked.

"You're going to think it's strange."

Napoleon encouraged me. "No," he said. "Go on."

"What I liked most was being followed."

"By the 'bad' guys?"

"The 'good' guys! I had to pace myself so I wouldn't lose my tail. They were my backup. For me, it became a kind of art form. I saw too many agents who didn't pay attention to their support troops. They ended up alone and stranded. Sometimes dead."

"How'd you avoid losing your 'good' guys?"

"How did I keep them with me? I left a trail of bread-crumbs," I teased.

"Well, this is America. Now, you'd have to leave a trail of money."

I looked at the clock. Eight-thirty. I glanced toward the door, and Jefferson was there. Jefferson was still an enigma to me, but at least he was prompt.

He had a broad grin. "I found the letters," Jefferson announced. "You were right. They're in the Taliaferro-Cole house."

"What room they in?" Napoleon asked.

Jefferson was too ebullient to let the tone of Napoleon's question bother him. "In a special room, on the second floor, at the top of the staircase. The room has no door handle."

"If there's no door knob, how do people get in?" Napoleon asked.

"The man who lives there..."

"Parke Hollingshed."

"Yes, the man who is writing the book about the letters. He tapped some sort of code into a plaque on the wall. There were numbers written on the plaque. Then there was a click and the door suddenly opened."

"Electric locks," Napoleon said, looking at me. "What numbers he tap in?" he asked Jefferson.

Lines appeared at the corners of Jefferson's eyes. "I don't remember. It all happened so fast."

"Well, those numbers are important," Brad said. "They're his identification code. If he taps out the right code, the electronic system opens the door for him; if not, he doesn't get in."

Jefferson sat on the edge of the couch. "Amazing! What would Benjamin Franklin have thought about all this?"

"Ain't modern science wonderful?" Napoleon commented wryly.

"I, too, was interested in things scientific when I was alive." Jefferson sat reflecting on remembered scenes from a distant past. "Scientific and agrarian," he added. Then Jefferson began to make observations about the events and great minds of his time. "I loved learning. For most of my life, I read an average of ten hours a day."

"Well, Jefferson, you got another opportunity to put your great mind to work," Napoleon said. "Find out what code this Hollingshed uses to open the door. Then we have a chance to help you." Napoleon gave Jefferson instructions on codes. "Beside numbers, there are two other buttons on the pad. A star key and a pound key." Napoleon showed him what they looked like on my telephone. "You let me know if he presses those, too."

"I'll get the code and bring it back here tomorrow," Jefferson said.

I looked at Napoleon thinking this was his cue to call off the whole operation. "Sure!" was all he said. He surprised me.

"Eight-thirty?" Jefferson asked.

"I might not be here," I told both of them.

Napoleon looked at me strangely. Jefferson's face also showed a similar note of reluctance. Neither of them felt comfortable dealing alone with each other.

"Kate's operation," I explained. Napoleon understood. "Napoleon, you have a key," I said and thought, "Jefferson, you don't need one."

Napoleon picked up on Jefferson's silence. "You willing to meet alone with a nigger? Two equal partners in this heist?" Jefferson stiffened. "Apparently I must!"

"Eight-thirty then," Napoleon said.

Jefferson hesitated. "This means you both will help?"

"We take it one day at a time," Napoleon answered, "but so far, so good."

Some of Jefferson's stiffness disappeared. He left the room by the staircase whistling something sounding like a Scottish reel.

"What happened to not stealing no letters for no ghost?"

"Can't make up my mind," Napoleon answered. "Don't know if I want to help the sorry dude or not. Only thing I do know is I have to watch your back for Miss Kate. Anyway, we bought some time 'til he gets us the code." Napoleon's eyes twinkled. "Maybe by then, you come up with a plan."

"I thought white folks' plans got you into trouble?"

Napoleon smiled. "It happened, but we see what your plan is before I say 'no.'"

I had been thinking. "If they wired a single room for security, what about the rest of the house?"

"Good point! How we get in then?"

I picked up my invitation to the Christian Historical Trust's Halloween Party. "We could go in the front door on Thursday night, as their guests."

Napoleon pondered this. "Mean we have to get costumes."

"You game?" I asked.

"Maybe," Napoleon answered. "I want to think about this. Don't want to make no snap decision with the next ten to thirty years of my life hanging in the balance."

"You don't have to decide until Thursday night, but if the answer's 'yes,' we're going to need costumes for the party."

"I tell Chili. He'll get them for us."

Chapter Fifteen

Someone once said Man is the only animal who knows he is going to die. I don't believe it's true, but if Man, in general, spent as much time thinking about his mortality as I did, it's a moot point. In the few, isolated moments of reflection on the subject, my only conclusion was to live every day to its fullest. As to deeper theological matters, I relied on my innate shallowness to get me through.

I had also avoided, to an extent amazing even to me, the related subjects of hospitals and operations. Such is the unspoken fear within me. But VS Hospital is hard to avoid when you approach it from the I-95 turnoff. It has a presence, as my mother used to say. The hospital itself takes up several square blocks of downtown Richmond. Then it spills over to adjoining office buildings and houses. It is a large teaching-hospital of uneven reputation. Some departments are among the best in the nation; others are to be avoided. Gynecological Oncology is one of the jewels. Women come there from every state in the Union.

"Whatever happens," Kate said on the drive to Richmond, "I feel like I'm in the best hands."

"I'm impressed with Cipriano," I added.

"You're prejudiced. You told me you thought she was 'perky.'"

"Perky people can be impressive, too," I answered.

As we left the highway, VS Hospital loomed in front of us. Kate said. "I just hope I don't become a burden."

"I have a hunch we're going to be old and grey before either of us becomes a burden."

There was a pause, then Kate answered. "Brad, I hate to be the one to tell you, but we *are* old and grey."

"Fifty and fifty-eight are not 'old and grey' ages. I'm talking about eighties and nineties old and grey."

It was barely light outside. The street lamps were still lit. We parked in the hospital's lot and walked into Admissions. They pointed us to the pre-surgical unit on the eleventh floor. It was precisely six-thirty when we arrived at the nurses' station. A cute nurse named Brenda took us to a private room with a single bed and its own bathroom. Brenda was "cute" I told myself, but she wasn't "perky." Brenda gave Kate a pill. "A mild sedative," she explained. Then she had Kate go into the bathroom and change into a hospital gown for surgery.

"Very stylish," I said when Kate returned.

"You better be nice. Someday this might happen to you."

"A problem? With my ovaries?" I avoided the "C"-word.

"An operation, silly."

Kate lay in the hospital bed. We held hands. Kate had left her jewelry at home as the hospital's pamphlet had advised. I had the clothes she wore in a brown paper bag. She looked surprisingly grey and indefinably fragile lying there without her makeup. There didn't seem to be anything else for us to say.

After a short time, Dr. Cipriano's assistant, Inge, arrived, smiling and full of energy. I gave Inge the rating "Perky-in-Training." She took Kate's pulse. "By the way," Inge said, holding Kate's wrist and watching the second hand of her watch sweep along, "we got the result of your blood test this morning. It was an eight."

"An eight is good, isn't it?" Kate asked.

"*Great* news! Now, we've been known to get false negatives from this test, but the read-out is a very good sign. Dr. Cipriano wanted you to know this before surgery."

After Inge finished, she asked me if I was going to wait.

"Of course!"

"Then go down and check in at the Visitors' Lounge. I'll call you there from the operating room as soon as I have anything to report. Now, the operation could last as little as one and a half hours, but it could be longer," Inge explained. "So don't worry! Just let them know at the desk where you'll be."

"Good luck!" I said to Inge.

She turned at the door. "I've been Dr. Cipriano's assistant for four years. Your Kate's in very good hands."

"Kate said the same thing on the drive here."

"Well, she's right!"

A few minutes later, two interns helped Kate from her bed to a gurney. The resident nurse had already started an IV which was transferred with her. I bent down and kissed Kate, first on the forehead, then on the lips. I knew this was no time for tears, but I certainly felt like crying. Kate held my hand. "Take care of yourself," she said.

"You're the one having surgery."

"But I have a team of professionals taking care of me. You'll have to manage by yourself."

"Until you come back."

"Until then."

* * * * *

In the Visitors' Lounge, a grey-haired black woman with thick glasses like Ella Fitzgerald's smiled at me from behind her desk. She wore a neatly-pressed Sunday church dress and had to have been in her late seventies. "And which patient are you waiting for?" she asked.

"Kate Whitney."

She ran the eraser of her pencil down a long list of names. "Surgery with Dr. Cipriano?"

"Yes."

"Dr. Cipriano is very good," the woman said.

"And she's also perky," I added.

The woman looked up at me over her glasses like a school marm. "My name is Mrs. Wilson," she said flatly. "I'll be on the desk until one o'clock. It's best if you sit in the Lounge. If you go any place, even to the bathroom, you let me know. Understand?"

"Yes, ma'am."

"My name is Mrs. Wilson."

"Mrs. Wilson." I couldn't help myself. "I'm going for breakfast," I told her, "but before I go, I just want you to know I think you're 'perky' too."

The laugh came from her ample belly. "Perky? I'll show you perky, young man."

* * * * *

Breakfast was cafeteria style. I had scrambled eggs, bacon, hash browns, and a cup of remarkably bad coffee. The breakfast cost one dollar and eighty-nine cents. I reasoned the low price was really a new marketing ploy by the hospital's coronary care unit.

After breakfast, I returned to the Visitors' Lounge. I could hear Mrs. Wilson saying "perky" under her breath as I passed. She didn't bother looking up. I sat in a chair near the back of the room and finished *The Washington Post*'s crossword puzzle and then read the *Times-Dispatch*, all before eight. I had brought some bookseller's catalogues with me, but I had no desire to concentrate on them. There were a few magazines on a table. I finished the ones I wanted to read by nine-thirty and the rest by ten-fifteen. There was still no word.

After notifying Mrs. Wilson, I went back to the cafeteria and got a second cup of coffee which I took back to the Visitors' Lounge. When I returned, I asked Mrs. Wilson if she had heard anything.

"No, honey, I sure haven't. But don't you worry none. Your friend's in good hands."

Good hands! Good hands was becoming my mantra.

By eleven, I could feel the level of panic rising within me. It was ten after eleven when Mrs. Wilson called my name. I went to her desk and she handed me a phone.

It was Cipriano's assistant, Inge. "We're taking a longer time to finish than we thought," she told me. "I just wanted to let you know."

"Are you finding...anything?"

"No. The doctor's still examining the area, but so far everything looks fine. The mass was an enlarged fallopian tube. It was left when Mrs. Whitney had a hysterectomy twenty years ago. We've removed it and sent it to the lab for a biopsy. It's a precaution but if it were cancerous, Dr. Cipriano would have seen it by now."

"Did the doctor have to make a standard incision?" I asked. "Dr. Cipriano mentioned it was a possibility."

"No, she's still working with the laparoscope. Unless something changes, Mrs. Whitney might be able to go home this evening."

Finally, I felt guarded optimism, like a basketball team ahead by ten points with two minutes to play. There was confidence building, but I knew some menace could still be lurking a moment away. I couldn't shake the shroud of tension and worry hanging around me like a dense cloud of moisture. Obviously, I had worked with Bruce Hogarth too long.

But I had to share my news with someone and Alida's name was the first one to pop into my mind.

"Well?" Alida bellowed savagely, no doubt in an attempt to will good news.

I gave her my report.

"Whatever happens, see if you can get them to keep her overnight," Alida said after I had finished. "She doesn't need a long ride to Williamsburg on top of surgery."

"I'll do my best." And I would, because disappointing Alida was far worse than arguing with doctors and insurance companies.

If we had a second Temperance Movement in this country, I would hope they'd keep the axes out of Alida Pendragon's hands.

"And if you fail and they do send her home," Alida said. "Call me!"

"We'll be fine, Alida," I said reassuringly.

"This isn't about 'we'. Kate's the one who needs care. So don't be a horse's ass! Call me!"

I promised I would.

My panic was subsiding. I still wasn't ready to concentrate on work, but I couldn't keep thoughts of Jefferson and his letters out of my mind. I didn't reach any conclusions sitting in the Visitors' Lounge, but in a disjointed and unorganized way, a plan was beginning to emerge.

Dr. Cipriano called at Mrs. Wilson's desk just before twelve. "Everything went very well," she told me. "I gave her a thorough examination while I was in there and I found no cancer."

I breathed deeply. "It took a long while," I remarked.

"Longer than I expected. It was a large mass to remove laparoscopically," she hesitated. "Inge did tell you it was an enlarged fallopian tube?"

"Yes."

"And then I removed the ovaries and fallopian tube from the other side. They were left after the same hysterectomy."

"An untidy doctor?"

"Not really! It was standard procedure back then. Nothing I found had any sign of disease, but there's no use taking chances and having to go through all this again."

I agreed.

"But the good news is there was no cancer," Dr. Cipriano concluded.

"Yes, wonderful news!"

"It is," Dr. Cipriano said. "And you have no idea how infrequently I get a chance to give it."

"When a patient gets to you it's usually fairly late in the game, isn't it?"

"Yes! But it's part of the territory for a cancer surgeon. Your's is the first happy call I've been able to make in the last ten days. It's why I live on such a high energy level. It keeps me from being depressed and makes me *perky*."

"Has Kate been talking in her sleep?"

"She might have mentioned something," Cipriano said, laughing.

I handed the phone back to Mrs. Wilson.

"Good news?" she asked.

"Yes!"

"Usually is with a phone call. The surgeons most always come down in person if it's bad."

* * * * *

Kate was out of Recovery and into a private room of her own by two. The bed was slightly raised and a nurse was feeding her spoonfuls of ice chips.

"Dr. Cipriano said you're going to be fine," I told her.

"No cancer?" she mumbled.

"No cancer!"

"You're not lying to me, are you?"

I raised the middle three fingers of my right hand. "Scout's honor."

"Did they make the big cut?"

It took me a second to figure out what she was talking about. "No," I finally answered. "They did the entire operation laparoscopically."

"Good," Kate said.

"You can still wear a bikini."

"Don't make me laugh. I hurt too much!" Kate *was* in obvious pain.

The nurse asked, "On a scale of one to ten, how much are you hurting?"

"Six hundred!!" Kate answered.

"I'm going to call your doctor. See what we can do." She left.

"They really didn't find cancer?" Kate asked again once the nurse had gone. Kate sounded as if she had wads of cotton in her mouth and probably felt she did, too.

"They really didn't."

"Thank God."

"Already did," I said. "Kate, where do you hurt?"

"All the places you hurt when you've been run over by a large truck! The most terrible pains are in my shoulder."

The nurse returned with a needle in hand. "Morphine," she told Kate, who smiled.

"She's complaining about her shoulder," I told the nurse.

"Gas pockets," the nurse said quickly. "They pump a lot of air into the body cavity when they do laparoscopic surgery. Sometimes it gets trapped inside. She won't feel it by morning. Too bad she's allergic to aspirin. It usually helps. But meanwhile we can give her morphine so she can rest tonight."

"Does this mean you're going to keep her here?"

"It's been approved."

"Good! She'll be more comfortable."

The nurse looked up at me with an appraising glance. "Yes, she probably will."

I brought Kate's bag of clothes back up to the room and hung them in the small wardrobe closet. When I left an hour later, Kate was dozing, lost in a haze of morphine. But at least she wasn't feeling pain anymore.

Chapter Sixteen

I found a parking space in the pay-lot next to Merchants Square. I hated to pay my own landlord to park there, but I was in a hurry and running out of time. Colonial Williamsburg had an employee parking lot I could have used, but it was over a mile from the bookshop. My only alternative was the "free" lot next to Parker's Rare Books, but every time I was running late, there never seemed to be vacant parking spaces—Parker's Law.

I walked the four blocks to the Taliaferro-Cole House and managed to arrive at four-thirty. Parke Hollingshed was in the back yard watching workers erect a canvas tent over the L-shaped garden area.

"Brad," Hollingshed said absently, his eyes glued on three workers who were coaxing a final vertical support pole into a freshly dug hole. "We're expecting two hundred and fifty people tomorrow," he said.

"It's the social event of the season." I don't know if I succeeded in keeping the sarcasm out of my voice, but Parke didn't seem to notice. And why should he? For Parke Hollingshed, it *was* the social event of the season.

"You're coming, aren't you?"

"It's looking more and more probable," I answered.

"What?"

"Kate had an operation today," I replied. My remark had nothing to do with Hollingshed's question, but I allowed him to make the obvious inference. I should have gone into politics!

"Everything go alright?"

"Yes. Thanks for asking."

With the social amenities observed, we both watched the workers make final adjustments to the yellow and green striped tent, tweaking the various elements into place with the same grunting and jerks an overweight woman might use wrestling her body into a girdle.

"It's like a circus coming to town, isn't it?" Hollingshed said, still watching the workers and the tent.

"Not a bad analogy."

"I'm a writer!" Hollingshed said. "I'm supposed to spout good analogies."

"Speaking about writing, where is your book?"

Hollingshed grimaced. "We wanted to have copies available for the party, but there were the inevitable production problems— well, you know how it is."

Hollingshed turned and looked at me. "Brad, I've been babbling. How can I help you?"

"I know this isn't the best time to ask, but I was talking with Theodore Jay a few days ago about my mail order operation. He suggested I see how you organized the Trust's."

"Brad, it's the day before the party!" Hollingshed raised his hands, palms up, like an evangelist beseeching God. He looked around at the workers in the yard, as if they were all dependent on his supervision and blessing.

"If you're too busy, maybe I could just go in and look around by myself."

My remark either offended or frightened him. "Not possible."

"I wouldn't ask if it weren't important."

Hollingshed stood, shifting his weight from one foot to another. It was as if his entire body was involved in making the decision. "I only have a few minutes," he finally said.

"All I need."

The Taliaferro-Cole House is an odd structure for an eighteenth century building. Most houses of the period are perfectly balanced. Doors were placed in the center of a facade, and what was on one side of them was a reflection of what was on the other: the essence of Palladian design. Not so here. Both the front and rear doors were set off-center. This led to an awkward arrangement of rooms inside. We entered by the rear door. It led directly into the kitchen. We reached the stairs to the second floor offices by walking through the kitchen and dog-legging to the left. As we started up, I noticed you couldn't see any of the other rooms from the staircase because the sight lines were also slightly skewed. As a consequence, no one from another room could see the steps. In the Taliaferro-Cole House, the staircase was an utilitarian element of design, not something the architect wanted to show off.

"What exactly can I tell you about our operation?" Hollingshed asked.

"I want to explore ways to improve my mailing list, learn how to ship books cheaper," I answered.

When we got to the top the stairs, I saw the door to the hidden room Jefferson had described, the one with no door handle. It was slightly to my left. The electronic panel was on the far side of the door.

"I set up our mailing list program," Hollingshed said proudly. "At the beginning, before I was totally concentrated on writing the Jefferson book."

"Your book is almost ready for the public, can't you tell me what it's about?" I asked this as coyly as I dared, but knowledge is power.

Hollingshed playfully wagged his finger at me. "You're going to have to wait for a few more days like everyone else. All I can say, it's going to change people's thinking about our third President.

The book is going to be a sensation!"

He led me to the right, down a central hall and into an ample room occupying half the second floor. The room was a very efficiently laid-out office, with desks and computers for three, and a fourth work station in the corner, "for visitors," Hollingshed told me. He booted-up one of the computers. "We send a great deal of mail through this office. The computer contains thirty-two different mailing lists. Most of them are for fund-raising, but we have three separate lists for public relations announcements."

I must have looked retarded, because Hollingshed felt the need to elaborate. "Different notices get sent to radio and television, the general press, and Christian outlets. But the heart of our system is fund-raising. There are twenty distinct categories for mailings. Take our correspondence with individuals from the Christian Right. They hear a slightly different message than the academics do. One concentrates on religious and family values; the other on history. We also have regional mailings to let people know where Dr. Jay will be speaking."

"Jay said you send out a lot of packages," I prompted.

"Mostly to our principal donors. They're like premiums. They don't cost much, but they keep us in touch with our supporters and give them something tangible to remember us by."

"How do you send them?"

"U.S. Postal Service. Priority Mail. Those red, white and blue cartons in the corner. It costs three dollars and twenty cents to mail, but we haven't had one lost in the past year and a half."

"I use UPS," I said.

"So did we."

I nodded my head with the appropriate amount of awe and respect.

For a man who was short on time, Hollingshed lingered for the next hour, telling me everything I would ever need to know about his computer system, jumping from one program to another with lightning speed. It was no accident the Christian Historical Trust was rich. For most people, Hollingshed managed to list birth dates, wives, anniversaries, children's names, and other personal facts. Hand-addressed cards were mailed on appropriate days. The occasional newspaper article on a subject of interest was photocopied and sent with a short note. Husbands rarely give wives so much attention. If you were alone or troubled, you couldn't help but think the Trust truly cared for you, even if no one else did. It was all done so subtly, with warm, personal touches. The average contributor wouldn't suspect the Machiavellian, well-oiled machine laboring beneath the surface.

It was dark when I finally pulled myself away from Hollingshed. I walked to Parker's Rare Books. Bruce had already left. I made a quick call to Alida to tell her the hospital was keeping Kate overnight. Then I locked up. I didn't want to confront Jefferson. My thoughts about him were still muddled. Maybe I was really seeing his "chindi," the soulless evil left behind. Maybe the whole affair was a high-tech joke by the CIA. These thoughts gnawed at my insides like Thai food. If I were an oyster, I would have been creating a pearl, but being me, I was probably only shortening my life span.

Hopefully, Jefferson had learned the access code by now. He could tell Napoleon. I had other matters on my mind.

* * * * *

At ten-thirty, it was cold as I left my apartment. I was wearing a black turtle-neck sweater and dark trousers. I wished I had remembered my jacket.

I parked my car out of the way, off a dirt side-road, six blocks from the Mosley house. I didn't want the police to see it on a routine patrol of the neighborhood. This seemed like a good idea at the time, but as I walked the six blocks, gripping my flashlight, I realized the lameness of my strategy. I had no earthly reason to be skulking around, no excuse for parking my car where I did. If the police stopped me, I would be reduced to being a blathering idiot, a role I was eminently qualified to play. I almost turned around. Almost!

A full harvest moon bathed the road in a warm orange light. I didn't need my flashlight to walk, so I turned it off. Yellow police tape still circled the Mosley house. The front door was locked and sealed with a large day-glow police sticker. I walked to the side, to the door leading directly into what had been Peter's office. It was also locked but someone had forgotten the seal. I yanked off a piece of plywood the police had nailed over where the windows had been and opened the dead bolt.

Once inside, I turned on my flashlight and moved directly to the bookcase, groping with my fingers until I found the latch against the wall. The shelving unit rolled to the side once again exposing Peter Mosley's bookbinding laboratory.

A quick look told me Philip Norge had taken my advice and moved the books to safer quarters. Nothing else in the room seemed disturbed.

I heard the outside door creak. I turned off the flashlight. I could hear my heart pounding in the ensuing silence. There was a muffled thump followed by the sound of a pile of books falling over. I didn't move. I wasn't breathing either. Was it the police? I had no right being there. What I was doing was breaking and entering. Then another thought started my heart beating triple-time. Maybe Peter Mosley wasn't dead and was standing outside.

I must have stood still, a piece of a frozen tableau, for over two minutes. Beads of sweat formed on my forehead. In fact, my entire body felt clammy in the cold night air. I didn't hear another sound. I thought of those World War II movies where submarine crews tried to out-wait each other in total silence while destroyers circled above. I consciously slowed my breathing.

Even so, I was the first to stir. I figured if it was the police in the office, I was going to be caught in any event, and if it was Peter, I might gain the element of surprise. Cautiously, I crept around the corner, jumped to the center of the floor, and turned on my flashlight. Nothing! Then I heard the noise again. It was on the other side of the rolling bookcase. I walked around, flashlight in hand, ready to use it as a weapon if I must. I pointed to the spot where I heard the noise and lowered the beam to the floor. It was a cat, a large, black tabby.

"Get out of here," I hissed, more relieved than angry.

It scampered wildly around me and slithered out the door.

My hands were trembling. I waited until I had regained some control over them, went back into the bookbindery and grabbed a stack of the eighteenth century paper I had seen during my last visit. I was careful to add some of the other papers to the bin so its loss would be less apparent. I put my purloined paper in an envelope I was carrying beneath my belt at the small of my back.

I closed and relatched the bookcase. I took care to relock the door and to replace the plywood, reattaching it to the door using the original nail holes.

When I got to the car, I heard something brush against the branches of a tree. Again, I turned my flashlight toward the noise. There was a light-grey great horned owl sitting on a lower branch. With supreme confidence, he didn't trouble himself to stir when I shined my light on him. I stood still and we observed each other silently for several minutes. As beautiful as he was, the thought of police made me break off my nature study. I turned off the flashlight, threw the envelope with the stationery on the passenger seat, and drove away.

Chapter Seventeen

By eight the next morning, when I got to the hospital, Kate was already dressed.

"I have to tinkle," Kate said. "Then they'll let me go home." She sipped water through a straw with the unconscious zeal of freshmen at their first fraternity party.

"You look good," I told her.

"Except for the pain around the incision, I feel good."

"No more achy shoulder?"

"Went away in the middle of the night."

"Good," I said.

"I'm really looking forward to going home," Kate told me between sips of water.

"Home is but a tinkle away," I reminded her.

* * * * *

Alida was sitting in front of Kate's apartment when we arrived an hour and a half later. Kate smiled her warmest smile when she saw Alida, but she winced getting out of the car. Kate walked more gingerly now than she had in Richmond. I wondered how much of her earlier good spirit could have been credited to residual morphine. For whatever the reason, Kate's *bon hommie* was beginning to fade.

Alida was holding a brown paper bag.

"What did you bring?" I asked.

"Chicken soup. What else do you bring a patient home from the hospital?"

Alida stayed with Kate while I went to the pharmacy to have her prescriptions filled. With waiting for the insurance company to approve their portion of the payment and traffic, it was an hour before I returned. Kate was already bedded, in flannel pajamas and a silk robe, a mostly empty bowl of chicken soup beside her on the night stand.

"You get my pain pills, big boy?" Kate said, straining to be upbeat.

"I know the way to a girl's heart," I replied.

"And I know when it's time to leave," Alida said. At the door she squeezed my forearm. "Take care of her," she said. Then as an afterthought, she added, "You're both very lucky."

Kate was asleep within fifteen minutes of taking her pills. I washed the dishes and generally straightened up. I had unplugged the bedroom telephone and was glad I did when the one in the kitchen rang an hour later.

"How's Kate?" Napoleon Robespierre Jones asked.

"Sore, but good. She's sleeping now."

"Glad it wasn't the Big C."

"So am I, Napoleon. So am I."

Napoleon hesitated. "We still on for tonight?"

"Was Jefferson able to get the code?"

"We got it." There was irritation in his voice.

"You don't sound very pleased."

"Jefferson's a royal pain. He don't think too highly about black folk, is all," Napoleon replied.

"You think you're imagining it?" I asked.

"If I imagining anything it's ghosts! Prejudice I've seen all my life. I know prejudice when I run across it, even in the world of spectral images!"

"What do you want me to do?"

"Tell me I ain't crazy." There was a long pause.

"You probably are crazy. I'm probably crazy, too."

"You no help!" Napoleon paused again. "Since I was a kid, I felt the fool working for the white man. No matter how nice they treat you on the surface, inside they think of you as different. Now I'm about to do something could get me thrown back in stir. Why? To help out some damned-fool-honky-bigot-ghost?"

"Definitely crazy," I replied.

"You comfortable with stealing letters like he wants?"

"No!"

"Didn't think so."

"Napoleon, you're free to back out," I said, and meant it.

"Then who's going to watch your back?" Napoleon asked.

"I'll be fine."

"What Chili told me, too! Something happen to you, Miss Kate will be on my ass for the rest of my sorry life."

I laughed, but it was probably true. "Were you able to get costumes?"

"Chili just left to pick them up in Richmond."

"Richmond?"

"Closest place. He said we lucky we could get any costumes, it being Halloween and all. I told him to drop them off at Kate's apartment when he gets back."

"What time?"

"Five. I'll come over. Oh," Napoleon paused. "Almost forgot. Chili say he got us a horse-drawn carriage to take us to the party in style. Pick us up at eight o'clock by Parker's Rare Books."

"Christ, Napoleon, a carriage? We want to blend in with the crowd."

"You going to do something real stupid like this, you might as well do it first class," Napoleon replied.

He had a point.

* * * * *

I spent the rest of the afternoon thinking about Jefferson and his letters. I made a phone call asking for help with the plan forming in my head. It was a very iffy idea. I wasn't sure, even then, Napoleon and I would actually follow through, but by five o'clock, I had the concept's rough outline all framed out. It wasn't much. If I had proposed it when I worked for the CIA, I would have been laughed out of my job. But the plan did satisfy most of the objections Napoleon and I had, and there wasn't any time to come up with a better solution. Hollingshed's book was to be released the week after the party. If we were going to do anything, it had to be tonight.

Kate was still napping when Napoleon arrived. I spent a few minutes filling him in on the details.

"Ain't bad," Napoleon commented when I finished. "Ain't bad at all." Napoleon folded his arms across his chest and closed his eyes. At first, he sat on the couch, then he lay down on it, eyes open, staring at the ceiling. "Course we have to sneak up the stairs without anybody seeing us."

"A big 'if,'" I acknowledged.

"And hope they didn't change the code for the vault. And then there's all the time we have to wait afterwards."

"All true!"

Napoleon sat up again. "Yeah, I like it!" he said, smiling and slapping his hands together. "'Course I also liked the plan got me invited to spend some time at Sewell."

"Who's out there?" Kate called from the bedroom.

"Moi," Napoleon shouted.

"Well, come on in and give me a very light hug," Kate shouted through the door.

We walked into the room and I stood there as Napoleon and Kate carried on a conversation in French, a perverse language invented to intimidate me.

After a few minutes, Napoleon said, "Brad, you look surprised a black man can speak a foreign language!"

"No," I answered, "I'm surprised *you* can."

"It's how we met, after all," Kate said. "Napoleon, Chili and I in the same classes at *Escoffier Ecole*, learning how to cook in the French manner."

Somehow I had never equated Napoleon living in France with his learning the language. A linguist like Henry Higgins could have devoted a lifetime analyzing Napoleon's English. I wondered if Napoleon's French was similarly garbled, and how it sounded to a native Parisian.

"Chili been reading about the school all the while we were in Sewell," Napoleon said. "A week before we got released, Chili tells me he has this wad of money he put in stock when he was on the outside six years before. Intel! Said the stock earned him more money while he was sitting in stir than he ever made working on the outside. Then he asked if I wanted to go to Paris with him, learn French cooking, come back and open a restaurant together. Hell, it beat any plan I had, hands down."

"They liked Chili at *Escoffier*," Kate added. "They offered him a job teaching nouvelle cuisine, but by then the three of us had agreed to start Chez Bayou."

The doorbell rang. I left Napoleon and Kate in the bedroom. Chili was there holding a four foot stack of clothes and boxes. I grabbed half the parcels before everything fell to the ground, and together we took the piles into the living room.

"The costumes are there," Chili said. He started walking toward the door, but before he could reach it, Napoleon emerged from the bedroom.

"What you get us, Chili?" Napoleon asked. Chili raised his left hand in a sort of wave and kept on moving. "Hey!" Napoleon said in a slightly louder voice. "What you get us?"

Chili stopped and let out a sigh. Napoleon went over to the pile of clothes on the sofa and started going through them. "What's this?" he asked, picking up a pair of red-sequined high-heeled shoes.

"There weren't many costumes left," Chili explained.

Napoleon raised the shoes to the level of his head and pointed at them.

"I got a Mad Hatter costume for Brad," Chili said. "You know, out of *Alice in Wonderland.*"

"Mad Hatters don't wear shoes like this," Napoleon said, holding them higher.

"No," Chili admitted.

"Then what's this?"

"Part of your costume," Chili answered.

"Who am I supposed to be?" Napoleon asked.

"Alice in Wonderland, herself."

Napoleon looked at Chili and then back at the shoes. "Alice in Wonderland? Chili, I going to kill you!"

"Later," Chili said. "Can't stay! I'm too busy being nice to my new pot boy, unnerstand?"

"Chili!" The name came bellowing from deep inside Napoleon, but Chili had already shut the door behind him.

Kate stood just outside her bedroom. "What's going on out here?"

"Chili brought costumes for us," I answered.

"Costumes?"

"Napoleon and I are going to the Christian Historical Trust's Halloween Party tonight."

"You're what?" Kate's glance went from me to Napoleon. "Why in the world? No! On second thought, I don't want to know. Not now, anyhow." She turned back to her bedroom. "You leave the pain killers in here?" she asked.

"On the night table, your side of the bed," I called after her.

"Good! I'm going to take two, and then I'll have a nice, quiet nap. Maybe later both of you can explain this to me."

Chapter Eighteen

"Ain't goin' wear no goddamned dress!" Napoleon snorted. We were in my office at Parker's Rare Books getting into our costumes for the party. Chili's carriage was scheduled to pick us up in a half hour.

"You can still back out," I reminded Napoleon.

"I told you, I the official back-watcher in this organization!" Napoleon tugged and hefted the dress around his body. I was afraid the dress was going to spring apart like the lid of a Jack-in-the-box. Its maker had not envisioned a six-foot-five-inch, two hundred and eighty pound Alice.

My costume fit perfectly. I was able to line the inside of my enormous hat with the blank stationery I had stolen from Mosley's house.

Napoleon saw himself in the bathroom mirror. "Shit," he said. "I look more like Martha or one of the Vandellas than I do Alice in Wonderland." Napoleon stopped to glare at me. He placed the blond wig on his head, the hair touching the five day growth of beard Napoleon normally sported. Chest hairs rolled over the neckline of the dress; hairy arms and legs shot out, like appendages from hell. "Okay, I wear the dress," Napoleon muttered, "but I don't wear no high heel shoes!" It was a compromise he had mentally worked out with himself.

"Wear your Reeboks," I told him.

"Reeboks? To a formal party?"

I stopped tying my shoe laces and glanced up at him. Napoleon was serious. I concentrated again on my laces to avoid laughing. "Not to worry, Napoleon," I said. "They're you."

Out of the corner of my eye, I saw Jefferson standing in the doorway.

Napoleon saw him too. "You say one word, I walkin'!" he shouted at Jefferson.

Jefferson ignored him. "What are you doing?" Jefferson asked me.

"We're getting dressed for the costume party at the Taliaferro-Cole house."

"Is tonight the night you're going to steal the letters?" he asked.

"Tonight's the night."

"But we have planning to do. I've spent the last day outlining the maneuvers." He reached into his jacket pocket and took out a folded sheet of paper. "I have assigned each of us a role to play in the destruction of the letters. I...."

I stopped Jefferson in mid-sentence. "We're putting ourselves at risk tonight," I told him. "We've come up with our own plan."

"Well, if you don't want to hear what I have to say," Jefferson said through pouting lips, "at least tell me what you've come up with."

"No!"

"No?" Jefferson started pacing back and forth across the office. "But this is my affair! It's my reputation at stake here!"

"And it's our ass!" Napoleon shouted.

Jefferson finally stopped and stared directly at Napoleon. "You look ridiculous!" he said.

"Ain't doing this for you, Jack! I'm here to watch Brad's back."

"I will not be called 'Jack' by a...." The sentence hung, unfinished, in mid-air.

"Darkie?" Napoleon suggested. "Nigger? Slave? Just what word you people use back then?"

Jefferson turned to me. "And why won't you discuss your plan with me?"

"Because I don't trust you," I replied.

"You what?"

"I don't trust you," I repeated in a calm voice. "I don't have much experience dealing with ghosts, so I'm having a hard time understanding just what it is you're after here."

"After? I told you! I want these scurrilous forgeries destroyed. I want to save my reputation from these false charges!"

"But the question I'm asking myself is, are these letters forgeries or are they genuine?"

"What?"

"Maybe you'd like us to destroy them because you don't want history to discover you for the traitor you were."

Jefferson's eyes widened, his mouth hung open. "You don't really believe I would have....?"

"Why not? It's just as believable as the story you concocted. Right now, standing here tonight, I'm simply not sure."

"You, sir, are a villain!" Jefferson shouted.

"And what are you?" I shot back. "Normal people die; they're gone, but you remain. Why?"

My question seemed to take the fight out of him. He sat on the couch, his elbows on his thighs, his head held between his hands. "I don't know the answer. I fully expected to be buried at Monticello, between my wife and my best friend. I do not know why I have been forced to endure this lengthy existence in Williamsburg, but I am attempting to make the best of it."

"And I'm attempting to make the best of you," I answered.

Jefferson stood. "Then we have nothing further to discuss!"

"I believe you're right, sir!"

Jefferson folded his arms across his chest.

"We'll both have to wait and see what happens," I suggested.

"You brought me hope," Jefferson said. "Now you dash my hopes in pieces on the ground."

"It's too early to say," I replied. "My plan just might work."

"No, sir! It will fail! Disaster can be the sole, inevitable result of your madness."

"You the one with madness!" Napoleon shouted.

Jefferson turned toward him, "And the word we plantation owners used when I was alive was 'nigra.'"

"Nigra?" The word exploded out of Napoleon and then he began to laugh. "Jefferson, for a spindly, white ghost, you do have a 'tude."

"You, sir, I'm sure, have a 'tude too—whatever means the expression!" Jefferson replied. He turned, and with all the dignity a former President of the United States could muster, Jefferson walked through the wall and out of my office.

"Yo' mamma!" Napoleon called after him.

Chapter Nineteen

⁕⁕⁕

"Who the hell are you supposed to be?" said Alfie Roberts, our carriage driver. He was staring at Napoleon Robespierre Jones in disbelief.

"I'm goddamned Alice from goddamned Wonderland," Napoleon answered. "You want to make somethin' of it?"

"You look more like one of the Vandellas," Roberts said. "You know the ones used to sing with Martha. No! No! You look more like Ru Paul—Ru Paul as a werewolf—but definitely Ru Paul."

I locked the door to the bookshop and tried not to look in Napoleon's direction.

"Chili rent your costume?" Roberts asked Napoleon.

"You think I get this for myself?"

Roberts laughed. "Oh, Chili! He's got some sense of humor!"

"You might want to tell everybody at his wake how funny he was," Napoleon said. "I'm sure he'd 'preciate it."

Alfie Roberts was in his "fancy" carriage driver's costume complete with powered wig. He was in his early thirties and had worked for Colonial Williamsburg since he graduated from high school. Driving people to and from special events provided him with extra income.

I sat next to Napoleon in the back of the carriage. Throughout the ride he emitted a low growl. Otherwise, we rode the two and a half blocks to the Taliaferro-Cole house in silence. There were six blazing cressets along the front of the house, set securely on poles in the grass between the street and the sidewalk. Their light bathed the front of the house in a warm, flickering, orange color. It looked like an artificially-lit set for a movie. The temperature had dropped to the mid-forties and I was sure the outside staff took comfort in the added warmth the fires brought.

The wood in the cressets emitted a pleasant, primitive odor evoking images of a time long past, one which disappeared in the Eastern United States before anyone, now alive, was born. The smell of the burning wood reminded me of it. Somehow, the odor was remembered in my genes or in some other unknown sense organ linking us humans, one with each other, one with the past. As our carriage got closer, I could hear the quiet strains of a jazz band playing under the yellow and green canopy in Hollingshed's back yard.

Hollingshed didn't need the tent tonight. The sky was radiantly clear and free from humidity. The moon was full enough to leave black shadows under the trees on the Duke of Gloucester Street as we drove along it. This was a perfect night for a Halloween party.

When we got closer, I could see there were ten attendants in front of the house, eight men and two women. They were all dressed as Indian servants complete with turbans, saris, and the like. The men had saffron colored sashes tied loosely across their waists and long swords hanging in scabbards from their hips. The Christian Historical Trust had paid attention to details and had spared no expense.

It was just eight-thirty. The party had officially begun at eight. Already there was a din of voices coming from the garden, a muted counterpoint to the music of the jazz quartet. As Alfie Roberts pulled the carriage to a stop in front of the house, I could see the musicians playing in the corner of the backyard.

Two of the attendants carried portable steps to us and I climbed out. Once on the ground, I automatically reached back to offer

Napoleon my arm for support. Napoleon ignored the gesture. He had raised the front of his dress over his knees to better see the steps and clumped down them, unassisted, his feet encased in white Reeboks with black trim.

Two different attendants escorted us into the house. The one with me asked, "Your name, sir?"

"Brad Parker."

From behind, I could hear Napoleon being asked the same question.

"I'm goddamned Alice from goddamned Wonderland!" Napoleon answered loudly.

"Mr. Brad Parker and guest," my attendant announced.

In the small entryway, Theodore Jay sat in an ornately-carved chair with red satin cushions. He was dressed as a Rajah and had a perpetually bemused smile. He might have been trying to project a casual assuredness, I had no way of knowing, but whatever he was attempting, it failed. His smile took on the appearance of a taut, nervous smirk.

To his right, Parke Hollingshed stood in a sort of son-of-Rajah costume. He seemed more relaxed and pleased. This was, after all, his party, assembled to celebrate the publication of his book. It was a party he had organized in every painstaking detail. From my first impression, it seemed to have all the early attributes of a great success.

"Congratulations," I said to both of them.

I don't think Theodore Jay heard me. He was now staring open-mouthed at Napoleon as Alice.

Hollingshed managed a polite "thank you" in reply to my remark. If he noticed Napoleon, he gave no sign. But by then there were people behind us waiting to be announced. As we were led off by new uniformed attendants, I saw Theodore Jay's gaze following us. He whispered something in Hollingshed's ear. Whatever he said made Hollingshed appear very serious.

Napoleon and I were herded through the kitchen to the garden outside. To our right, a long table, draped with white linen, served as a bar. Napoleon headed toward it. He surveyed the liquor bottles behind a row of bartenders, each dressed in a white shirt and black bow tie. "Tonight I'm drinkin' Absolut Vodka on the rocks," Napoleon said to one of the younger and more earnest bartenders, "with a twist of lemon squeezed against athe rim of the glass."

"Yes, sir."

"Now, you're goin' watch me. You see my glass getting near empty, you make me another." Napoleon palmed a twenty dollar bill and handed it to the young man. Where he had hid it in his costume was a mystery.

The bartender looked in my direction.

"Nothing," I said.

"A couple of these'll make the party go a lot smoother," Napoleon suggested.

"I got work to do," I said. "And I think we better do our job quickly before security finds us."

"You think they got security here?" Napoleon asked.

"Rutherford Talon does." I pointed to the corner of the garden where Talon stood, his two bodyguards, one on each side of him, standing slightly behind, scanning the crowd. "And the man over there with a cell phone, the one with the Indian outfit. Probably hired to keep out the riff-raff."

Napoleon had finished his first Absolut and the bartender had another waiting for him. "Good man," Napoleon said to him.

"I need your help at the bottom of the stairs," I told Napoleon.

"Now?"

"Now!"

We walked up three steps and into the kitchen. The entrance to the stairwell was obliquely off to the left. I headed straight toward it. There were two men and a woman standing in the hall next to the steps. The men wore tuxedos and cheap five-and-ten-cent-store plastic masks. As Napoleon walked passed, he managed to bump the senior man's arm spilling his Absolut over the man's white shirt front.

"Oh, my," Napoleon gasped. He took a white handkerchief from the front of the Alice dress and started to dab at the stain.

I didn't stand around to watch the rest. I took the steps two at a time and, a moment later, stood quietly in the dark hallway on the second floor. I waited at least three minutes, until my heart stopped pounding, until I was confident Napoleon's diversion had worked. No one had followed.

My eyes accustomed themselves to the dark. Still, I removed my pen-light from the inside pocket of my costume's jacket and flicked the switch. I needed it to see the security pad on the door, and I didn't want to trip over anything as I crossed the hall.

I heard a board creak under my foot as I walked toward the room Jefferson had mentioned, the one with the handleless door. I stopped, turned off the pen light, and waited again. No one came.

I was beginning to feel embarrassed and foolish just standing in the darkened hall. I knew enough about breaking and entering to realize this was not a good mental attitude. Even G. Gordon Liddy must have had more confidence in his maneuvers at the Watergate than I did then. Too many things had to go right for my plan to work.

I had managed to get up the stairs without being followed. Now, I was about to tempt fate for a second time. I tapped the code we got from Jefferson on the pad at the far end of the door. Jefferson could easily have gotten the code wrong; Napoleon could have transposed numbers; and there was always the possibility CHT changed their codes every few days. I thought of all this as I hit the final "pound" sign. Then I heard a hollow, metallic click and saw the door open.

I went into the room quickly. The door seemed to want to

close behind me, so I propped it open with a waste basket from inside. The room was a windowless vault. I worried the door was connected to a master panel somewhere and security was now aware someone had entered. I tried to work as rapidly as I could.

I ran my light along the walls to get a sense of how the room looked. There was a "V" shaped work station in the center, complete with computer, seventeen inch screen, laser jet printer, and telephone. In the far right-hand corner was a cabinet on which a small photocopier sat. Grey, metal bookcases were placed against the walls. These were filled with books, paper, and the usual office supplies—curious items to be kept in such a secure place.

I finished my cursory examination before I shined the light toward the bookshelf in the left-hand corner, where the letters were to be. I faced another of the great "ifs" with my plan. Jay or Hollingshed could have taken the letters and put them in a bank vault until the party was over. It would be the end of my sleuthing if they had. If the letters had been mine, I would have removed them. Instead, a grey archive box with metal corners sat in the spot where Jefferson said it would be. I opened the lid and saw a stack of letters inside, written on the same stationery I had stolen from Mosley's bindery. Each sheet was in its own protective, plastic sleeve.

I hadn't expected this. I was hoping for a quick grab-and-switch.

I thumbed through the stack. The correspondence was there, letter after letter, all signed in the distinctive hand of the third President of the United States. I wished I had time to read them, but I didn't.

I took off my large hat and removed the blank sheets of Mosley's eighteenth century paper I had safely inserted in the lining. The paper had survived its hiding place remarkably well. There was a slight curl to the leaves which I straightened by gently rolling the papers in the opposite direction.

Then, I went through the letters. I removed a random sampling from their plastic sleeves and replaced them with my blank sheets. I didn't take any of the letters from the first fifth of the stack. There was always a chance Jay might show a few of them to chosen board members. I reasoned he would pick letters from the top of the pile. From the remainder, I removed letters selectively, trying not to take more than two in a row. In the end I had replaced thirty-two letters with my blank leaves. It took a god-awful amount of time. I was sweating profusely despite the cold. I could feel my costume sticking to my skin like a wet bathing suit on a cold summer's morning.

I put the unused blank leaves back in my hat and set it on my head. Then I returned the remaining letters and my blank substitutes to the box which I put back on the bookshelf. I looked around to make sure I wasn't leaving any tell-tale signs of having been there. Then, I walked out of the vault with the thirty-two letters in my hand. I returned the waste basket to its former place.

I waited outside, not breathing. If there was a separate code to re-lock the room, I didn't know it. The door closed excruciatingly slow. I let out an audible exhale when I heard the dead, metallic click reactivate the system. Next, I hurried down the hall to the main CHT office where I found the empty Priority Mail envelopes where they had been the previous afternoon. I quickly put the letters in one of them and removed the strip of plastic on the flap, exposing the adhesive. I sealed the letters inside and took a neatly typed address label from my pocket along with a three dollar and twenty cent stamp. I put both of them on the envelope, which I buried half-way down in a full bag of outgoing mail.

I was back in the hall, almost to the stairs, when I heard noises from below and heavy feet clumping up the steps.

In the dark I saw the flashlight first. Behind it, one of the men shouted, "Hold it right there!"

I did. A second man came up the stairs and turned on the hall lights. Both men wore Indian servant costumes. The man with the flashlight was holding a thirty-eight service pistol in his right hand, and he was pointing it at me.

"Hey, you don't shoot people around here for trying to find a bathroom, do you?" I said, trying to put a slightly inebriated slur on my words.

"Harry, see if he's carrying," the man with the gun said.

"Jesus, George," Harry replied. "The man's looking for a john."

"Do as I say!"

Harry walked over to me, shoulders sagged, and performed a cursory pat down. "He's clean," Harry said to George.

George put his pistol away. "No one's allowed on the second floor, sir." His tone considerably altered.

"I really have to take a piss," I said. I gazed blankly ahead keeping my eyes unfocused.

"Over here." Harry opened a door across the hall from the vault. He even turned on the bathroom light.

"Thank you," I said and walked uneasily passed George. I was sorry I hadn't had the drink Napoleon offered. I had the look, but not the odor, of a drunk. George didn't seem to notice.

Inside the bathroom, I did what had to be done and then allowed the two security guards to escort me downstairs and out to the garden. I saw Napoleon at the bar talking with a young woman carrying a straw basket. I started toward them.

"Take it easy on the booze," I heard George say behind me.

"Took you long enough," Napoleon said as I approached. "Success?"

"Yes!"

"Want you to meet a new friend of mine. Brad Parker, this is Goldilocks."

"Hi," I said.

"You look like a man could use a drink," Napoleon suggested.

"Tanqueray on the rocks," I replied. My nervous system was not going to be satisfied with weak substitutes.

"Mother always told me, never trust a man who drinks gin," Goldilocks said.

"Your mother was probably right," I replied.

Napoleon pivoted, and with a series of efficient hand gestures, gave my drink order to his personal bartender.

"The Mad Hatter's an interesting choice for a costume," Goldilocks said.

"Goldilocks teaches in the Psychology Department at William and Mary," Napoleon explained.

Goldilocks was very attractive, probably no more than twenty-eight. She had a mischievous and provocative glint in her eye when she asked questions, daring the askee to reveal more of himself than he normally would. I could see Napoleon was enjoying the challenge. Conversation with Goldilocks, I had a feeling, was a competitive sport.

"Sorry," I said, answering her question. "No subconscious meaning. The costume was rented for me by someone else."

"Goldilocks thinks my outfit brings out the feminine side of my personality," Napoleon added.

"You are a most interesting man," Goldilocks said to him. Then she looked toward the house. "I'm going to find a ladies' room, but I'll be back."

"I'll be right here," Napoleon called after her.

Goldilocks walked away with what I thought was a slightly exaggerated hip movement, but exaggerated or not, it was effective. Napoleon mumbled "Oh my!" as he stared after her.

"Fine back watcher you turned out to be," I said.

"Watchin' that girl's back right now," Napoleon said. "She sure can walk!" He kept his eyes and attention on Goldilocks until she disappeared from sight. "Now, as to your back. When you were upstairs, I saw those Christian Trust security types running around the house. I figured they be looking for you. Didn't want to make it easy for them, so I came out here. Met Goldilocks."

"I noticed."

"If I would have stayed where I was, they would have caught you. But I didn't forget you. Figured if you didn't come out of the house soon, I'd go rescue you. Was giving you one more drink before I made my move."

"Well, I hate to ruin your love life," I said. "But I think we should leave."

"Leave the party?"

"Security caught me on the second floor."

"Thought you said you were a success tonight?"

"I was finished before they came."

Napoleon's eyes narrowed, deepening the lines in the corners of his eyes. "Why they let you go?"

"I told them I was looking for a bathroom."

"They believe you?"

"Maybe. At least they were unsure enough to be polite, but there's a good chance they'll check their valuables—see if anything's missing. I don't want to be around if it happens."

Napoleon's gaze strayed to the door where Goldilocks had disappeared. "Why do *we* have to go? Why not, *you* go—*I* stay?"

"I'm afraid of walking from here to the shop alone."

"Halloween got you spooked?" Napoleon asked.

"If I'm alone, there's a better chance they'll stop and search me. And if they search me, they'll find the blank sheets of paper in my hat."

"What'll it prove?"

"Nothing in a courtroom, but they would put two and two together."

"Damn!" Napoleon muttered. "You sure picked a fine time to get the jitters." He gazed longingly at the Taliaferro-Cole House's back door.

"Maybe the three of us could leave together," I suggested.

Napoleon grinned while considering the possibility.

When Goldilocks appeared again, Napoleon met her in the middle of the path. I was alone, studying the crowd. Rutherford Talon still stood in the same corner of the garden with his bodyguards close by his side. After three sweeps, I finally found George from the second floor. He was standing under a tree, staring directly at me with a cell phone in his right hand. I had no doubt I was being watched. I gulped the remainder of my gin.

Napoleon returned smiling. "Three of us leavin' together," he announced.

Our carriage wasn't expected for another hour, so we walked down the center of the Duke of Gloucester Street, putting distance between ourselves and the lights and sounds of the masquerade ball. The street was dark and deserted, and the Bruton Church graveyard was ahead of us on our right. I felt better having their company. Napoleon was right. It was Halloween and I did have the jitters.

Apparently I wasn't the only one. "I'm scared," Goldilocks said in a frail voice.

Napoleon reached over and linked arms with both Goldilocks and me. "We off to see the Wizard," he said, and before I could think or say anything, the three of us were skipping down the Duke, singing, laughing, and deftly sidestepping the horse droppings randomly decorating the cobblestone street.

Chapter Twenty

I have never been good at waiting. Temperament? A character flaw? I don't know, but after the Trust's Halloween Party, I now had nothing to do but wait. Results were going to take time. It was like baking a loaf of bread.

My chances for success were good if you factored in human nature. People normally relax after a major event like the Trust's party. I was counting on it. Still, too many "ifs" had to fall exactly right for my plan to work. If the Christian Historical Trust didn't investigate my presence on the second floor too carefully; if they didn't notice the Jefferson letters were missing; if they didn't look through their mail sack and find the package; if the post office...; if.... Now it was up to fate. I no longer had control—I never did. Control is an illusion we use to avoid facing our own insignificance.

So I busied myself with the mundane, beginning with fixing breakfast for Kate on Friday morning. She asked a number of questions about the party, most of which I wasn't ready to answer.

"Were you really there?" Kate had said at one point.

"I was working," I answered vaguely.

"Book business?"

"Related to the book business."

My reluctance to discuss Jefferson, my activities at the party, and the situation in general ignited Kate. In an hour she managed to list fifteen of my shortcomings and ten ways I had failed in our relationship.

"We don't have to continue," I finally said.

"I'm trying to decide for myself," Kate replied coldly.

Her remark left me unsettled and empty. I felt like a cracked. undecorated Polish easter egg reject, with the white and yoke sucked out of it.

By nine, Kate had taken two more pain pills. She was asleep before nine-thirty.

* * * * *

At eleven, I was in the Briar Wood Funeral Home where Alida had arranged a memorial service for Abbe Mosley. The room was embarrassingly empty. Seated in the middle were four people: three wearing red Ferguson Real Estate jackets, and a heavyset woman who looked to be in her early thirties. I found out later Abbe had recently sold her a house.

Sitting in front with Alida was a well-scrubbed woman wearing a grey pants suit in a style popular a decade earlier. She was young, no more than thirty, with a brusque tension in her gestures and a boyish, no-nonsense haircut, which seemed to compliment her overall presence. She looked vaguely familiar but I couldn't remember where I had seen her before.

Alida had arranged for an Episcopal priest, a Father Humphreys, to conduct the service. Humphreys had fine white hair, which flowed gently over his head, like a field of wheat on a breezy summer's day. He could have been an Episcopal priest in a Norman Rockwell painting.

The service was short. Father Humphreys stood behind a tiny altar holding the urn with Abbe's remains inside. He read from *The Book of Common Prayer*.

Father Humphreys had obviously never met Abbe. His "personal" remarks were read hesitantly from notes Alida had prepared. When the service ended, taped organ music came over a speaker system. The four mourners left quickly, glad, no doubt, to be enveloped again by the day-to-day activities of the living.

The priest went over to Alida and her friend. Suddenly, I remembered where I had seen the young, strident woman. *The Virginia Gazette* had published her photograph recently. Her name was Bonnie something, and she was in charge of a new home for battered women in Williamsburg. Perhaps, I thought, Alida had found another outlet for her energy and heart.

After Bonnie had left, I approached Alida.

"How's Kate?" she asked.

"Taking pain pills and sleeping," I replied.

Alida gave me a quizzical look.

"Things are tense between us."

Her face wrinkled with concern. "People react in strange ways when they come face to face with the imminent possibility of their own death," she said.

"I think it might be more. At times, Kate seems so distant. She looks at me as if I'm an escaped biology experiment from a high school lab."

Alida laughed. "You sure you're not borrowing trouble?"

"I don't know, Alida. I don't think so."

"Did you talk to Kate about this?"

"Just a little sparring around the edges."

"If she's running away from your relationship, avoiding the subject isn't going to solve anything. If I were you, I'd talk to her, Brad. I wouldn't wait. Things like this don't go away. They fester."

I drove back to Parker's Rare Books, swimming in emotions. I knew Alida was right, but I wasn't sure if I could handle a confrontation with Kate right now. So much had happened recently. Once again I felt scared, floundering in deep water.

I thought again of Jefferson living in an inexplicable half-world, neither heaven nor hell. I hated imagining Abbe walking around Williamsburg in limbo. At the very least, she deserved the peace in death which had eluded her in life.

I tried to remember incidents or traits about Abbe Mosley, my quiet tribute to her. Nothing came to mind. Nothing except the morning she brought me the Jefferson letter. I really didn't know Abbe Mosley at all. It embarrassed me.

*****

I spent the afternoon with Kate. She looked much improved after her nap. It was good again between us, as if the morning hadn't happened. We talked about childhood, likes, dislikes, impressions. At three, Napoleon brought lunch from Chez Bayou. "We got a lot of things to discuss," he said to me. Then Napoleon heard Kate stirring in the bedroom. "But not now!"

"When then?" I asked.

"I'll be in touch," Napoleon answered.

As he pulled out of the driveway, I thought I saw Goldilocks sitting in the passenger seat of his red, three-year old Pontiac Firebird.

"Let's take a vacation in January," Kate said. She had a travel magazine on her lap as we ate. "I should be completely recovered by then. Want to escape with me?"

"January is a good time. It's a dead month for the bookshop," I agreed. "Where do you have in mind?"

"I was thinking about Florence, Italy."

"Not Miami Beach?"

"Peasant! Florence can be very romantic."

"Florence can also be very cold in January."

"Are you sure?"

"Cold and damp."

"Have you been there in January?"

"No."

"Then how do you know with such certitude?"

"I just know," I replied.

We spent the next hour talking about other vacation spots—some where we had been, others where we wished to go. It was idle talk. "Florence in April?" Kate suggested.

"April is the New York Antiquarian Book Fair."

"The book fair's four days, not all month. We'll work around it," Kate said.

I was a coward. I didn't bring up our problems. I started to but felt foolish. Everything was so good and natural between us then. Alida might be right. I knew we would have to talk sooner or later, but for now I didn't want to "borrow trouble." Her feistiness could just be a reaction to surgery. Perhaps, I needed to be more patient and give her space and time to work out her problems.

By four, I could sense a change in Kate. She seemed to lose interest in our talk of vacations. Her energy level visibly flagged. At four-thirty she took two more pain pills and headed back to bed for a nap.

I went to the bookshop.

When I arrived, Norge met me at the door. This was becoming a too frequent habit. I wondered how long he had been there. "I just thought you'd like to know, we identified the corpse from the fire," he said.

"Who was it?"

"Mosley! We found old army dental records."

"Mosley was in the army?"

"I don't think it was his finest hour," Norge said. "He was given a general discharge. You can't really tell anything with general discharges. The relevant facts stay buried in army paperwork. But I *can* tell you, they don't give out general discharges for petty offenses."

"What about Anthony Calvado?" I asked. "You think he had anything to do with Mosley's death?"

Norge sneered. "The district attorney requested his extradition from New Jersey. We should know something by tomorrow. We have a lot of people hoping to see the reptile squirm."

"Look, as much as I'd like to continue this," I said, "I am expecting a caller."

We shook hands before we parted but both of us hesitated before we did.

Once inside the shop, I didn't have to wait long. Jefferson appeared in the office doorway at six-thirty.

"Well?" he demanded.

I was correcting galley proofs for my next catalogue. "Well, what?" I answered, returning to my work.

"You know what!" Jefferson was livid. If he could have grabbed me by my shirt collar and pulled me to my feet, I'm sure he would have.

"You mean, what happened to your letters?"

"I assume you took several," Jefferson said. "About a third were missing when I checked this morning."

I put down my pen and gave Jefferson my full attention. "Yes, I removed thirty-two."

"Why didn't you take them all? Damn you!"

"Because we live in a country of laws. Some of which you wrote." I peered over my half-glasses. "Stealing letters would have broken several of them."

"And stealing only a portion of them wouldn't?"

"I didn't steal them."

Now Jefferson was annoyed. Splitting legal hairs must have become popular with more recent American presidents. "You're not making any sense!"

"I didn't steal the letters. I didn't remove them from the premises. I didn't destroy them. I don't have them in my possession." Did I sound like William Jefferson Clinton, or what?

"Then what did you do with them? Did you just leave them there?" Jefferson paced, gesturing wildly.

"Yes."

I don't know if our third president had cursed during his lifetime, or if Jefferson had learned this skill in the years since he became a ghost, but he ably exhibited this talent for me. As he wound down, Jefferson asked, "Where in Hades did you leave them?"

"In the mail sack, in an envelope addressed to Alonzo Galbraith at the Library of Congress."

Jefferson seemed confused. "My library?" he asked.

"It's a little bigger than it was when it was 'your library'," I said.

"What does this Galbraith do there?" Jefferson demanded.

"He uses science to determine if documents are authentic."

"But they are! My God, Citizen! You must believe!"

"It's not what I believe, it's what Galbraith must prove."

"But you just left the letters there, in the house! Might not someone notice and intercept the package?"

I shrugged my shoulders.

"Your Mr. Galbraith might never see them!"

"It's possible," I answered.

"Then wh-wh-why?" Jefferson stammered. "Why did you do it?"

"Because I couldn't think of a better plan!" I shouted back. Jefferson had pissed me off.

"But these letters are obvious forgeries. If Mr. Galbraith is a true man of science, he will vindicate me." Jefferson paused. "Did you think I would actually give my country back to the British? After all I went through for independence?"

"I think it's a possibility," I answered. "Parke Hollingshed thought it was a possibility, too. He spent two years of his life writing a book based on them. If the letters are genuine, I wouldn't want to go down in history as the man who destroyed them."

"But what if the letters never get to your Mr. Galbraith?"

"Then you were right and my plan failed."

"And my fate rises or falls on this flimsy confection of your mind!" Jefferson stopped pacing. "You should have consulted me!" he screamed.

"Why?"

"I could have advised you! I could have devised 'the better plan' which eluded you! Damn you! I was one of the leading intellects of my time, and you didn't even bother to ask my opinion!" Jefferson sat down and lowered his head. "So I am in the hands of fate," Jefferson concluded.

"We all are," I said. "Every day."

Jefferson ignored my philosophical insight. "And so I must wait," he muttered.

"Waiting has always been difficult for me, too." I could give Jefferson no further comfort. I had no answers for either of us.

"When will we know?"

"If everything goes well, Galbraith should get our package on Monday," I answered. "He promised to work on the letters immediately. We should know something by Tuesday or Wednesday."

"I will be back then," Jefferson said. "You realize I am the one who will suffer the most if the letters remain unread by your Mr. Galbraith. You should have left the planning to me."

"But I didn't."

"No sir, you did not!" Jefferson left by the door this time and walked down the stairs with the stiff pride of a prisoner awaiting the guillotine.

Chapter Twenty-one

Everything started to unravel on Saturday, including me. Kate and I finally did have our talk.

"What's wrong?" she said. "I don't know. Sometimes I think it's you, sometimes me. All I know is I'm no longer comfortable with 'us.'"

I stuffed my rising emotions back into the deep recesses of my mind and tried to be analytical. "Specifically what's bothering you?"

"I'm not going to present you with a laundry list."

"You know I want to work this out between us," I said. "I love you."

"I know," Kate said, "it makes it harder. For now, I just need time alone to figure out what I really want."

"You don't solve problems with a relationship by yourself, Kate."

"You might not but I do."

I could see this conversation was causing Kate as much pain as I felt. "Well, how much time do you think you'll need?" I asked.

"I don't know. This isn't the type of thinking you can put a time limit on."

"Generally. Are we talking a day? A week? A year?"

"Brad, don't push me on this! I've had a serious operation. I have a business to return to. I won't be able to even start thinking about our relationship for another six months."

I could feel my anger. "And what do I do in the meantime?"

"It's up to you!"

This conversation was definitely not going well. I was so frustrated I couldn't get another sentence out.

"I'm going to take my time to think about what *I* want," Kate continued.

"Maybe we could see a marriage counselor."

"We're not married."

"I think we need some outside help. I feel you're circling the wagons and there's no room inside for me."

"I'm not spending money on counseling! Most of my married life I put up with crap I didn't like! I'm not going to again."

"Nobody's asking you. If something bothers you, we can talk about it. Maybe I can change; maybe you can alter your attitude."

"My attitude's not the problem here," Kate said.

"What is? All I've got so far is you don't like the way I keep the bed sheet loose around my feet and you resent it when I use large bath towels."

"Well, I like the sheets tight and what you do makes that impossible." Kate stood. "And as far as the towels, they take up too much room in the washer."

"Christ, Kate! These are not things to break up a relationship over!"

"And furthermore, I don't like your language!"

Bingo! I began talking louder, my vocabulary reduced to army barracks doggerel. This led to Kate storming into the bedroom, slamming the door behind her.

I find arguments like this have movements like a crazed piece of theatrical ballet, forever escalating to a manic, fevered crescendo. So in the parlance of the theater, I exited stage-right: I escaped to the bookshop.

* * * * *

Things at the shop were no better. Bruce was in a horrible mood and I wasn't up to coping. I holed up in my office with the door closed.

At one o'clock, Philip Norge arrived with an entourage of uniformed and plain-clothes police. I was still in my office, once again unsuccessfully trying to understand the vagaries of my computer, when Bruce called me downstairs.

"What's this?" I asked, looking around at Norge and the five other men huddled in the middle of my shop.

Norge excused himself and walked toward me. He put his arm around my shoulders and used his bulk and strength to herd me into Bruce's shipping room.

"What the hell have you gotten yourself involved in?" he said in hushed tones.

"I haven't a clue what you're talking about," I answered, but in truth, I had guessed.

"This morning before ten o'clock—on my day off, I want to point out—I had already talked with my police chief, the Governor of the State of Virginia, and a gentleman named Sigmund Byrd."

"Byrd?"

"Who happens to be the Associate Director of the F.B.I." Norge stood in front of me, his arms draped, one each, over my shoulders, his face no more than a foot from mine.
"And do you want to know what they told me?"

Norge didn't look as if he expected an answer so I didn't offer one.

"They told me there was strong evidence you stole thirty-two letters written by Thomas Jefferson from the Christian Historical Trust, and they instructed me to come over here and find them." Norge moved back a half step. His hands were now on my shoulders. He began to gently knead them. "What is it with you and Thomas Jefferson letters?" he asked.

"Phil," I began, speaking in the same low tones as Norge, "I did not steal thirty-two Thomas Jefferson letters."

"You sounded like a lawyer just then, so I'll rephrase the question.

If you didn't steal the letters, do you know where they are? This is your window of opportunity to tell me before we start looking. We have a signed search warrant, and as you see, I have the manpower. Eventually we'll find them."

Bruce walked into the shipping room, probably drawn by talk of Thomas Jefferson letters. "Christ!" he exploded. "I mailed the letter to Mr. Stanley myself and it didn't come back! I see all the mail! I would know! The Postal Service probably lost it."

"This doesn't concern Peter Mosley's letter," Norge told him.

"Captain Norge thinks I stole thirty-two Jefferson letters from the Christian Historical Trust," I explained.

"Thirty-two?" Bruce looked at Philip Norge as if he wasn't wearing trousers. "This is the most absurd thing I've ever heard! Thirty-two Jefferson letters? I doubt we had four in all the time I've been working here."

"This isn't a debate!" Norge said, his voice raised in frustration. He turned to me. "Your last chance to make it easy on yourself," he said in a more modulated tone.

I remained silent.

Norge motioned to his five detectives. "You can start now." Norge turned and smiled at me, "We'll find them."

"Not here you won't," I replied.

"I also have warrants to search your apartment, Chez Bayou, the apartments of Napoleon Robespierre Jones, Chili Rodriguez, and Kay Whitney, and the homes of Alida Pendragon, and Bruce Hogarth."

"My home!" Bruce barked. "I take back my earlier remark. *This* is the goddamned most absurd thing I've even seen!" Bruce plunked down on his stool to fume.

I looked out the door and saw a uniformed policeman there. "What's he supposed to be doing?" I asked Norge.

"Keeping customers away from the premises until we finish."

"Oh? Well, you might have a warrant to search my shop," I said. "But you don't have a court order to close my business. This is a prime sales day. It's the last home football weekend for The College of William and Mary."

Norge's face turned scarlet. His blood pressure must have been in the stratosphere. He was certain I had stolen the Jefferson letters, but he knew he had no authority to shut down the business.

"Okay," he agreed, "but I'm taking you over to the police station for questioning."

"I'm not talking to you or leaving this shop unless I see legal papers saying I must!"

"We'll see," Norge said.

"Yes, we will." I called Jonathan Ward, my lawyer and reached him at his house. He had just come back from the golf course. After I explained the situation, he asked to speak with Norge.

I couldn't hear what Jonathan said, only the tone in which he said it.

After they finished, Norge was more subdued. We reached an uneasy compromise and spent the rest of the afternoon awkwardly trying to stay out of each other's way. Miss Manners would have been proud of us both.

At one point, Gordon had come down from my office to stand on the counter and survey the chaos.

Norge looked over at him.

Bruce noticed this. "You going to search his litter-box, too?" Bruce asked.

"A good idea," Norge replied with Calvinistic seriousness. "Harvey, check the cat's litter-box."

Harvey was in shock. He scowled at Bruce. I played my role, pointing to the litter-box which sat in the corner of the downstairs bathroom.

At two, I got a call from Kate. When I had left the apartment, I thought she might never talk to me again, but there she was. The whipsaw effect in action! "Brad, there are policemen here. What's going on?"

"They have search warrants," I replied.

"But what are they looking for?"

"Captain Norge mentioned thirty-two letters written by Thomas Jefferson."

"And they think you have them?" Kate's voice was filled with incredulity.

"Apparently!"

"Is this part of the Halloween Party mystery?" she asked.

"Could be, but I can't discuss it now."

Kate reluctantly accepted this. "Oh, and before I forget, Chili called. The police are also searching Chez Bayou. Chili said they took Napoleon to the Station. Chili's very concerned."

I gave her Jonathan's home number and asked Kate to call him and get Napoleon released. "I'm sorry the police are doing this," I told her, "but it's all beyond my control."

"Brad, what is going on?"

I didn't have an answer I wanted to share.

* * * * *

Later, Napoleon called. "Your friend Ward is a righteous dude," he told me. "Still don't think the police know what hit 'em. You got cops there with you?"

"Captain Norge himself," I replied.

"See yah!"

I had been waiting to talk with Napoleon since the Halloween Party. I'd have to wait a little longer. I was getting accustomed to delay, trained as I was in spending time at doctors' offices with Kate.

The search was painstakingly slow. There is no better place to hide a book or a sheet of paper than in a bookstore. I was relieved to see the five men Norge brought with him took great care when sifting through the stock—amazing for people not used to handling rare books and prints. But no matter how careful they were, I was determined to go back through the inventory myself and present the Williamsburg Police Department with a bill for damages.

Customers drifted in and out of Parker's all afternoon. They looked curiously at the detectives at work, made their inquiries, and browsed. Surprisingly, no one asked what was happening, and Bruce and I didn't volunteer any information. We made a few nice sales, but we were nowhere near the volume we should have reached. Atmosphere is everything in a bookshop, and plain-clothes policemen mechanically examining every book and print in the place weren't conducive to sales. Thomas Jefferson had become a costly apparition to know.

When we closed the shop at five-thirty, Norge and crew were still busy with their treasure hunt.

I wasn't about to leave the police alone in the bookshop, and since there were other officers searching our homes, I could see no reason to force the issue. There was no escaping their presence. So I called over to Rustermann's and explained what was happening to Antoine. I ordered dinner for Bruce and me, and included a nice bottle of Clos Du Val Cabernet Sauvignon. In this case, living well *was* the best revenge.

Antoine himself, followed by one of his busboys, delivered the dinners.

"You should be ashamed of yourself!" he told Norge. "Accusing Mr. Parker of stealing letters!"

I saw Norge fighting with himself. He wanted to reply but thought better of it. Maybe a portion of his California cool was returning; maybe he was just feeling beaten down.

Bruce and I brought stools to the front counter and ate there. Antoine had even included a votive candle, which I lit. The shop's fluorescent lights overwhelmed any such subtlety, but style counts.

Bruce and I talked about books and customers, trying as best we could to ignore the search party and their clambering noises. While we ate, Gordon leaped up on the counter and I chopped up some of my quail and rabbit stew for him. He ate greedily before sitting near us, purring softly as he performed his after-dinner grooming. The search might have been an inconvenience for us, but Gordon was enjoying the evening immensely.

"I don't like the thought of policemen in my apartment," Bruce finally said during dessert.

I could see, despite the good dinner, Bruce was smoldering with worry, his Germanic mind conjuring up images of wreckage and doom.

Kate called a little after seven. "The police are gone. They left the restaurant, too."

"Good," I replied.

"Are they still with you?"

"Yep!"

"And you can't talk," Kate offered.

"Don't think I should," I explained. "They got a search warrant. Maybe they asked for a telephone tap at the same time."

"You mean they could be listening to us?"

"I don't know, but it might be a good idea to assume they are," I cautioned. I made a mental note to call Jerry Pollock and have him sweep the phone lines, shop, restaurant, and apartments for bugs. Jerry was a private eye in Hampton who collected biographies of colonial Americans. I knew very few people who weren't in the book trade or collecting one thing or another.

"Alida called about an hour ago," Kate mentioned. "The police were at her house all day. She's very angry."

"Not at me, I hope."

"Her anger is presently directed at 'the Gestapo state,' as she put it. Alida Pendragon thinks very highly of you."

"Me?"

"Yes, but she asked me not to pass it on because she was afraid you'd raise book prices on her."

"Ain't unconditional love grand?"

"She *does* love you!" Kate answered. "But it doesn't mean she *trusts* you!"

I told Kate I would stop in on her when the police finished their work. It was after ten-thirty when I saw Norge standing in my office doorway on the same spot where Jefferson had repeatedly materialized.

"Well?" I asked.

"You're a real, goddamned, cocky bastard, aren't you?" Norge said.

"Can I assume you didn't have any luck finding the letters?" Norge was silent.

"Don't be angry with me. At least I didn't remind you I told you so. Yet!"

"Sure! Wisecrack! But I damn well know you're guilty! There are too many coincidences for you not to be."

"Like what?"

"Like Mrs. Mosley offering you a Jefferson letter in the first place. Like you being in the Taliaferro-Cole House the day before the letters were stolen."

"You know precisely when the letters were stolen?" I asked.

Norge ignored my comment and continued. "And at the party, you were apprehended outside the room where the letters were kept."

"What room?" I asked.

"On the second floor."

"I was looking for a bathroom!"

"But why were you at the party in the first place?"

"Why? It was the social event of the season!"

"Parker, this isn't over," Norge said. "Sooner or later I'll nail you."

"Really!"

"From now on, you spit on the sidewalk, you're going to get a summons."

I took three deep breaths for effect. "You ever consider the possibility I didn't steal the letters?"

"Not for one goddamned minute!"

"Now all you have to do is prove it."

Norge treated me to his finest ghetto stare. "It's a matter of time, my friend. You are the only link in this mess."

"Don't be too sure. If you look at the Trust's bank accounts you might find another link to Mosley. Maybe you might find the Trust's letters and Mosley's are one in the same."

"And maybe you're blowing smoke up my ass," Norge said in a voice more hesitant and less assured.

"Check the bank accounts! It's something I would do. Especially if I had Sigmund Byrd of the F.B.I. breathing down my neck."

"Go screw yourself," Norge said and left.

Chapter Twenty-two

❧❧

Sundays are mine! While Parker's Rare Books is open, I'm not. It's my one free day and I guard it with the same care a desert traveller gives his water canteen.

Kate and I had a Sunday routine: sleep late, read the papers, and do minimal housekeeping—just enough to keep the health inspector at bay. Sometimes we attended church. The eleven o'clock service at United Methodist on Jamestown Road was a favorite. On other mornings we would just stay in bed and crash. No matter what else happened, we'd eat lunch out. It was Kate's attempt at market research.

I was sleeping alone in my apartment when the telephone rang at seven. I assumed it was Kate. I fumbled for the receiver. "Brad?" said a familiar voice, but the voice wasn't familiar enough.

"Parke Hollingshed!" the voice said. "Did I wake you?"

"Yeah."

"I'll call back."

"No! I'm awake now."

Hollingshed hesitated.

"It must be important or you wouldn't have called this early," I prompted.

"I need to talk to someone,"

I remembered the police. "Not on the phone."

"Where then?"

"I could come over to your place."

"My place is part of the problem."

I was suddenly curious. "Where are you now?"

"At a pay phone in the Visitors' Center," Hollingshed answered.

I considered the possibilities. "You have a car?"

"Yes."

"What if I meet you on the Colonial Parkway? Toward Jamestown. There's a place where you first see the James River, a big parking lot's on your right."

"I know it."

"Just beyond, there's a smaller lot to the left. I'll meet you there at nine-thirty."

I called Kate and told her about Hollingshed.

"I could cut Parke short and go to church with you," I said.

"Not today. I'm going to stay here, alone."

"Rustermann's at noon?"

There was a long silence. "Okay," Kate finally said.

I drove down the Parkway with the clear conscience of a man who didn't have to be in two places at once. The weather had turned colder. The air was crisp and vibrant; details of things far away were clearly visible without Williamsburg's usual shroud of humidity. I was five minutes early; Parke Hollingshed was already waiting.

"Let's walk by the river," he suggested, and we started down a path to a narrow beach. To me, Hollingshed had always been the epitome of waspish style: horn-rimmed glasses, close-cropped hair, neat buttoned-down collars, crew-necked sweaters, and khakis. As I walked behind him, I noticed an overall disheveledness terribly unlike Parke. His walk also had a uncharacteristic, jangly gait.

"What's bothering you?" I asked when we finally stopped at a tree trunk lying across the path.

Parke Hollingshed didn't look at me. He preferred staring across the James. "Something bad is happening at the Trust," he said, keeping his gaze on the far shore. "Where to begin?"

"The beginning?"

Parke told me the beginning was at the Christian Historical Trust's board of directors' meeting on the Friday morning after the party. Theodore Jay had opened the proceedings with a renewed swagger. The first order of business was the election of the next Chairman of the Board. Jay's name was placed in nomination along with Talon's. The board members voted by writing their choice on folded slips of paper, handed to Parke, who served as secretary for the meeting.

Hollingshed announced the results. "Talon six; Jay five." Hollingshed saw color drain from Jay's face. Jay immediately asked for a re-count. The result was the same. Finally, Jay insisted the board be polled orally. Each member stood and stated his vote.

"We came to Calvin Rusk. He looked defiantly at Jay and said 'Talon.' I thought Jay was going to have a stroke."

Apparently, Rusk had promised his support to Jay. In return Jay had given full college scholarships to Rusk's two grandchildren.

"Management perks?"

"It's one way Jay kept his chairmanship, I learned. Jay called Rusk 'Judas.' But Mr. Talon took charge before things got out of hand. He moved the vote be recorded. Those who had supported Talon seconded and approved the motion."

"So Jay was sandbagged by one of his own."

"Apparently. If Dr. Jay knew Rusk was in Mr. Talon's camp, he still had time to bribe another board member, but with Rusk's vote in hand...."

"He didn't have to."

"Within seconds there was a motion to hire a team of outside auditors who would review the Trust's financial records. It was approved six to five. Next, the board voted to deny Jay access to Christian Historical Trust records. When this motion carried, Dr. Jay stormed out.

"You must have been in shock," I said.

"I was stunned! Dr. Jay had been my mentor, the one who gave me a chance to write the Jefferson book. Obviously, Mr. Talon had a vendetta against him." Hollingshed still concentrated on the James. "Mr. Talon approached me after the meeting and insisted we talk later at his suite in the Colonial Inn. I didn't want to go, but I was afraid not to." Hollingshed sat on the overturned tree trunk. "Talon asked what my book was about. I assumed Dr. Jay had told him, but I was wrong. When I gave him an outline, he didn't like what he heard. I left before I was thrown out."

I paused and looked across the River at the spot where Hollingshed had been staring. Part of the United States Navy's mothball fleet shimmered in the water and sunlight. "Now's the time to talk, Parke! What the hell are these letters all about?"

For the next fifteen minutes, Parke Hollingshed told the story of a disheartened Thomas Jefferson secretly plotting with John Adams in the summer of 1804 to return the United States to George the Third and England.

Hollingshed went on, citing detail after detail, how letters were passed back and forth between Adams, Jefferson, and representatives of George the Third. He had an incredible number of facts to support his theories, and I listened for as long as I could.

Finally, I interrupted. "Bullshit!" Jefferson had been right about me, after all. Somewhere in my core, I *did* believe the letters were forgeries.

"Yes, and at the beginning I thought the letters were bullshit, too. But there's too much evidence they're not," Hollingshed said. "Every letter has a date and place. In every case, Jefferson was at those places on the dates indicated. There were five times when Jefferson had lengthy meetings with a messenger. On each occasion, historians wrote of Jefferson being alone, suffering from one of his migraines."

Hollingshed continued with evangelistic fervor. "And George's messengers came from London a week before their meetings with Jefferson and left two days later. I have ship's manifests, all sorts of collaboration. Back then people didn't sail across the Atlantic for a ten day visit! It all fits! One hundred and twenty-two letters and not a factual error in any of them."

"Where did the letters come from? Who owned them? How did they survive?" Questions flowed out of me.

"The letters appeared to be Jefferson's personal copies."

"Why would he keep them?"

"Why did Nixon keep the oval office tapes? Who knows! My guess is Jefferson wanted to document history."

"Then, where are Adams's letters to Jefferson?" I asked.

"Probably lost, like the originals he sent Adams. These letters almost were."

"Who found them?"

"Do you know the Washington-Carters?"

"You're not talking about the old man, Bill Carter, are you? The one who lives on Westfield Plantation?"

Hollingshed nodded.

"Parke, Bill Carter is senile. Has been for ten years."

"But his nephew, Artemis, isn't."

I had first met Artemis five years before. He sold me an early nineteenth century account book from one of the Washington-Carter plantations in the western part of the state. Artemis was in his late thirties, just out of the Army. Apparently, he preferred selling family papers and antiques rather than work.

Recently, Artemis had been appointed Bill's legal guardian. There had been rumors of his abusing Bill, reports of Bill rambling unclothed around the estate.

"So the Trust bought the letters from Artemis?"

"No, from Peter Mosley. Mosley acted as the Trust's go-between."

Jay had lied to both Norge and me.

"Did Peter borrow them recently?"

"No!"

"Parke, would you know?"

"Yes! I live at the Taliaferro-Cole house. With security and my being present, yes, Brad, I would know! Especially during the last three weeks."

"How much did the Trust pay for the letters?" I began to feel like Captain Norge.

"Two million dollars."

Knowing the participants, this was a shameless lie. "Two million dollars?" I repeated.

"We got clear title. Artemis signed a statement saying the letters had been in his family since Jefferson's death. They were handed down father-to-son, generation after generation, until they came to Artemis."

"How much of the two million did Artemis get?"

"Dr. Jay said one point eight million dollars."

I doubted Mosley would have paid that sum, and knowing Artemis, with even a fraction of that much cash in his pocket, he would have been as far away from his crazed uncle as he could get. Artemis, Mosley, Jay. Thieves, dealing with thieves, dealing with thieves. It was wonderful.

Hollingshed still appeared uneasy.

"Why *did* you want to talk to me?"

"I think I'm being set up as the thief, and I don't know how to protect myself." Now, Hollingshed faced me. "On Friday night, Talon asked if I had been to the vault during the party. We've been keeping the Jefferson letters in a locked vault room on the second floor."

I had the sinking feeling Hollingshed might soon be charged with a felony. If he were, the truth wouldn't set him free. Jefferson was the least believable alibi available.

Hollingshed continued. "The police questioned me yesterday, because several of the letters were stolen from the vault during the party."

"Well, had you been in the vault?"

"No!"

"Then why do the police think you were?"

"Because my pass code was used for access."

"Who knew your code?"

"Nobody! Pass codes are confidential."

Hollingshed needed a plausible alternative. "Did you ever write the code anywhere?" I asked.

Hollingshed slapped his forehead with the palm of his hand. "Of course! I had it in my address book."

"Under 'p' for pass code?"

"Under 'v' for vault."

"And people saw you using this address book when you went into the vault?"

"During the first few weeks, I just couldn't remember the damn code."

"If it's any consolation, you're not the only one suspected of stealing the letters."

Hollingshed looked at me blankly.

"The police were at my shop and apartment all day yesterday searching for them, too."

Now I felt I had done my duty. I had given Hollingshed a plausible explanation for how his code could have been used. It was a hell of a lot more logical than Thomas Jefferson's ghost stealing the code for a crazed bookseller. "And Parke remember, the police also might think you took a few of the letters yourself to test and see if they're genuine."

My remark seemed to slowly filter through Hollingshed's brain. "But the letters are genuine!"

"And having them checked by an expert just before your book came out wouldn't have been a bad move. Save the Trust embarrassment if you were wrong."

Hollingshed just shook his head. "What are you talking about?"

"Just talking! But you came to me for advice. My advice is 'stay loose, hang tough, and think positive thoughts.' Now is not the time to worry or panic. Good things are happening!"

"Christ," Hollingshed said. "You sound like a Chinese fortune cookie!"

Chapter Twenty-three

After meeting Parke, I made a long distance call outside the 7-11 on Jamestown Road. I talked for fifteen minutes.

Even with this delay, I was able to get to Rustermann's before Kate. When she arrived, Antoine doted over her. He was so glad to see her looking so well and happy.

As I listened I became aware of a presence standing next to our table. I looked up and saw Rutherford Talon and his two body guards, a massive clump capable of blocking out the sun.

"I don't want to interrupt your meal," said Talon, "but it's important we talk soon."

"When?"

"How about your bookshop in an hour?" he said. "I'd be grateful."

Talon's attitude was disarming. I agreed.

After he left, Kate asked. "What does Talon want?"

"I guess I'll find out."

* * * * *

Rutherford Talon, like Thomas Jefferson's ghost, was prompt. I didn't see his body guards but I guessed they weren't far. We sat in my office on opposite ends of the Chesterfield couch.

"I understand Theodore Jay sicced the police on you yesterday. I wanted you to know it was Jay, not me. By the time I found out about it, I was too late to stop the investigation."

"I never thought you would call the police to find those Jefferson letters," I answered.

"Why not?"

"Because you of all people would believe the letters were forgeries and worthless."

Talon smiled at me, but the smile didn't remain long.

"You look worried."

Talon hesitated, assessing my discretion. "The Trust. We're going over the books now. Theodore Jay apparently stole a great deal of money from us."

"How much?" I asked.

Unexpectedly, Gordon bounded into the room and jumped into Talon's lap. "We don't know exactly, but it might be fifty million dollars." As he spoke, Talon's hand automatically petted Gordon's head.

"Fifty million?"

"We knew he had been stealing, but no one imagined how much. Initial indications show how very slick he had become, moving money around in a now-you-see-it, now-you-don't shell game. We have the F.B.I. and Interpol working with us now, but the son-of-a-bitch had been doing this so long, I doubt if even he could trace the money back through the web he's created."

"I'm sorry for your problems, but that's not why you came to see me."

"No," Talon answered. "I came to ask you about Parke Hollingshed."

"What about him?"

Talon raised his eyebrows, first his left, then his right. It was a wonderful effect. "I think Parke Hollingshed stole the Jefferson letters."

"Parke wouldn't steal letters," I replied.

"Why not?"

"It's not in his nature for one thing. For another, he's a historian and he's trained to preserve the past not destroy it."

"What if keeping the letters meant proving his book was a forgery?"

"Then why not steal all the letters?"

"Perhaps he stole the more obvious forgeries, willing to take a chance with the rest. His code was the one used to go into the vault the night of the party."

"He told me the code was written in his address book," I said. "Everybody at the Trust knew it was there because he couldn't remember his pass code."

"How did you learn about this?"

"Parke came to see me this morning."

Talon raised his eyebrows separately again.

"He came to me for advise because he thought he was being set up as the fall guy."

"And what advice did you give him?"

I tried Talon's trick with the eyebrows, but it obviously took practice. "Stay loose; hang tough; and think positive thoughts. I suggest you might be well served to do the same for the next few days."

* * * * *

About three, I finally caught up with Napoleon at Chez Bayou. I told him the story about Hollingshed and Talon. Napoleon looked up at me from his late lunch of eggs and bacon. We were sitting alone in the main dining room.

"You understand, now's the time you got to watch your backside," he told me.

"Watch it for what?" I asked.

"For your Dr. Jay."

"Jay's probably five thousand miles away, in a banana republic with no extradition treaty."

"Don't count on it."

"He has the money. He knows CPAs are looking through the Trust's books. If you were Jay, wouldn't you be heading up river in Brazil?"

"I would," Napoleon said, "and so would you, but we not Theodore Jay! We didn't make up a bunch of letters just to 'dis' a dead white man."

"Might not be true," I said. "The letters still could be real. Parke Hollingshed's no fool. He thinks they are."

"Yeah, but Parke Hollingshed is a *believer*. He sees a brass ring when his book comes out. Can't grab it if the letters are fake. Jay knows this. My guess is Jay set him up to play the fool. Jay, he's a dangerous man!"

I sat silently watching Napoleon pick up a strip of bacon and fold it into his mouth. Bacon as finger food!

"I don't like it! Don't like it one bit!"

I stood. "Got to go."

"Just watch your butt! I knowed people like Jay at Sewell. Don't let him get behind you."

Chapter Twenty-four

❦

Bruce greeted me on Monday morning. "Man called, didn't leave his name. Said to tell you, 'the eagle has landed!' Cryptic or what?"

"It only means the United States Postal Service is doing a fine job!" I replied.

"I'm sure you'll explain some day," Bruce muttered and went back to his shipping room shaking his head. "Someday when I might not have to testify against you in court."

* * * * *

At ten-thirty, Bruce was on the intercom. "Rutherford Talon, line two. He's upset!"

"I need your help," Talon began. Bruce was right, he did sound upset. There was also heavy static on the line.

"Where are you? The South Pole?"

"On a cell phone outside the President's house. I need a favor. Fifteen minutes. I'll send Timothy around with the car."

I was finding Talon's requests hard to turn down.

Timothy was one of Talon's bodyguards. He drove with his eyes in constant motion, scanning the street in front and behind him. It was the result of good training. Timothy drove slowly and carefully, and didn't talk. He concentrated on what immediately surrounded him. His attitude reassured and unnerved me at the same time.

The scene at the President's house was chaos. There were five moving vans with Michigan license plates parked in front. A man with a fork lift was unloading pallets on the lawn. The pallets contained four foot high stacks of boxes held together with heavy shrink wrap. Talon followed a wiry black man in denim overalls. His arms flapped as he talked.

I saw Parke Hollingshed. "What's going on?" I asked him.

"My book," he replied.

I looked at the nearest pallet and saw the words, "Jefferson, the Traitor," written in a black marking pen on each box. "Jesus, Parke, how many copies are there?"

"Sixty thousand," he answered. "Twenty-five copies in each box, twenty-four hundred boxes, a little over forty tons of freight."

"And they delivered them here?"

"Dr. Jay's instructions."

Rutherford Talon saw us. "Sixty thousand copies!" he screamed over the noise of the fork lifts. "Sixty thousand copies!"

"Can't you find a warehouse?" I asked.

"No time. Didn't even know they existed until the trucks arrived a half hour ago," Talon said.

I looked at the darkening sky. "Can't the drivers put them someplace else? It looks like rain."

"Their orders call for outdoor delivery, and they're Teamsters," Talon said with a resigned disgust. "I thought you, being a bookseller, would have a suggestion."

"Sorry! I've never handled forty tons of books at one time before." I thought for a second. "Is there any room in the President's house?"

"The basement's dry," Hollingshed offered.

I looked up at the sky again. "A dry basement sounds good." I borrowed Talon's cell phone and explained our situation to Bruce. He called the fraternity house where our two part-time packers lived. Within fifteen minutes, we had a work crew of sixteen stretched in a line from the lawn to the basement. They handed the boxes one to another, working together with the speed and stamina of youth. Once the crew was working, I made a second call to Bruce and within thirty minutes, we had another sixteen man team moving boxes in a second line. Even so, it took over two and a half-hours to carry everything inside.

The rain held off until the last half hour. Before we finished, our clothes were soaked. To his credit, Talon stood outside with the rest of us, tearing plastic wrap from around the pallets. The man worked hard. At times his energy seemed to challenge the students'.

When the move was finished, Talon paid each worker a new fifty dollar bill Timothy had brought back from a bank.

"I owe you a large debt of gratitude," Talon said to me.

"For saving a bunch of books you didn't want in the first place?"

"It's not the books. I wouldn't want the weasel to think he could defeat me with his little trick." Exhaustion had replaced most of Talon's agitation. "Thanks to you we've averted a disaster."

"Sixty thousand wet books certainly would have qualified!" We were standing alone in the unfinished basement. Boxes of *Jefferson, the Traitor* were stacked floor to ceiling from the back wall to the steps.

"Jay changed the shipping instructions on Friday afternoon, after the board meeting. If this was the only mess he left, I would be fine, but between the two of us," Talon came closer and looked around the room to make sure we were alone.

"Jay's stolen money is long gone. The FBI, Interpol, and the IRS, they don't give us even odds on recovery. It's obvious Jay had been stealing funds for some time, moving vast sums through the Bahamas and Switzerland. The money's been laundered so many times, I doubt if even Jay himself could trace it all back to the Trust. By now it probably has frequent flier mileage."

"You have a plan?" I asked.

"Try to track Jay down, indict him, and then barter time off his sentence for returned money."

Talon's plan sounded as professional as mine did for taking the letters.

"Nobody's seen him since Friday," Talon said. "I doubt if he's still in the country."

"A friend of mine suggested Jay might stay around to exact revenge."

Talon did his trick of arching his eyebrows again. "Why?" he asked.

"My friend spent a good deal of time around criminals," I replied. "Personally, I think Jay's vanished."

Talon nodded. "Who knows?" His eyes remained pensive until he willed his smile to reappear. "Go home! Get some dry clothes. Timothy will drive. As I said, I'm deeply in your debt." He extended his hand which, like before, gently enveloped mine. "Do take care."

"You take care, too!"

* * * * *

Kate and Alida were sitting at the table in Kate's apartment when I came to change clothes.

"You look like a drowned cat," Alida said.

I explained about the truckloads of books. "Can't stay. Have my driver and a car waiting to take me back to the bookshop."

Neither of them were very impressed, which seemed my current lot in life.

* * * * *

I went back to Parker's Rare Books for two hours in the evening to give Kate more time alone to think. It's soothing to be in a bookshop at night. During the day, I have a thousand interruptions: telephone calls, customers, employees needing direction. At night there is none of this. I can sit alone with my books. I can concentrate solely on the one task I'm doing. The answering machine takes care of the telephone; all other distractions are outside locked doors. Aside from lying in bed with Kate after making love, sitting alone in my bookshop at night, with a cat asleep on my lap, is the closest I have ever come to total peace.

I had expected to see Jefferson, but he never materialized. He had left angry and hurt, so I was not terribly surprised, but I sat thinking about his letters.

I was removing people from my mailing list, those who hadn't ordered anything in two years. Gordon was asleep on my thighs. My thoughts drifted to the letters. I was torn. Part of me wanted the letters to be forgeries, vindicating Jefferson's memory as author of the Declaration of Independence, Renaissance man, Virginian, failed farmer. His "spectral image" had dispelled much of the myth for me. Still, I couldn't easily accept the historical Jefferson as a traitor. Still, another part of me wanted the letters to be genuine, wanted Parke Hollingshed to bask in the glory of his book.

Somewhere between the "G"s and "H"s I must have fallen asleep Kate was there, dressed as a gypsy fortune teller, turning over cards.

"Yes," she said. "Spontaneity! I like that in you, but I can't stand you not planning ahead! Generosity! But you seem incapable of saving money."

Kate turned over card after card. Character traits she once liked in me became flaws. It was unsettling. I woke up feeling used.

I picked up Gordon, cradling his warm body to my chest as I stood. Then, I gently laid his in my empty chair. He looked up and mouthed a silent meow before circling his body into a tight ball. He was asleep before I could turn out the lights. I envied his serenity as I drove alone back to my empty apartment.

Chapter Twenty-five

On Wednesday, I had a glimmering of hope my life would once again return to what passes for normal. It was wishful thinking. In reality, events were unfolding in unexpected patterns like images in a kaleidoscope. Although I still hadn't heard from Galbraith, "the eagle has landed" meant he had the letters in hand.

Kate had returned to work with a vengeance. On Monday and Tuesday we only spoke briefly on the telephone. During her recovery, Kate had concocted an idea of making Thanksgiving to New Years a Chez Bayou Festival. Each night would feature a different theme: a Peruvian Christmas, a Hawaiian Luau, some evenings with live orchestras, others with a classical guitarist. It was a grand, manic concept. Chili seemed excited by the challenge, but when I met Napoleon on the street, he just rolled his eyes. "Might not be alive when the year's over," he said, "but if it works, I'm goin' to die a wealthy man."

* * * * *

The first news of Galbraith came from a *Washington Post* reporter. Since I was an antiquarian bookseller from Williamsburg, she called to get my reaction to Alonzo Galbraith proving a newly discovered group of Jefferson letters were forgeries.

I can't remember what I said, but it wasn't terribly coherent. It's hard to be intelligible when the plans you set in motion suddenly take shape in the real world. I knew how Eisenhower must have felt on D-Day as the news of victory slowly filtered into headquarters.

After a few minutes, I asked the reporter questions of my own. According to her, Galbraith was able to prove absolutely the letters were forgeries. My hare-brained scheme had worked! I took a deep breath and tried not to shout for joy. Now wasn't the time.

My only regret was I didn't have anyone to share the moment with. Gordon couldn't understand, and Bruce Hogarth? Well, I didn't want to risk the whole story for fear he would just walk out? I thought of calling Napoleon, but thought twice. No doubt he was busy and he was never very interested in history in the first place. I even wished Jefferson would come by, something I had never thought possible, but he didn't appear either.

My name seemed to be on an informational bulletin board for the media. It was afternoon before the last newspaper reporter called. I poured a celebratory glass of Johnny Walker Black Label, the best scotch I owned, and toasted myself. Sad, but I was feeling too good to let it bother me.

An hour later Rutherford Talon knocked. "Did you hear?" he asked.

"No," I said and let him tell me. As he revealed the details, it became evident Galbraith had remembered my Sunday telephone call and had properly fabricated Parke Hollingshed's part in bringing the letters to him.

"So it was Parke all along," Talon said. "He wasn't satisfied the letters were genuine or Theodore Jay's authentications were valid. He went the extra mile and got this man, Alonzo Galbraith, to look into the matter. I haven't read Galbraith's report yet, but I understand it leaves no doubt they're fakes."

Talon paced my office like the ghost of Jefferson had before him. "Told you!" he bragged. "Told you it wasn't in Jefferson's character to be a traitor to his country."

I was about to remind him I had said the same thing about

Hollingshed, when I saw a sudden, pained expression tense the muscles around Talon's eyes.

"My God," he said, "what am I going to do with sixty thousand copies of *Jefferson the Traitor?*"

I didn't have an answer.

Gordon jumped up on my desk, and Rutherford Talon absent-mindedly patted his head as before.

"Well, I wanted you to know you were right. It wasn't in Parke's character to steal the letters anymore than it was in Jefferson's to write them. I'm glad it wasn't. Parke saved the Trust even more public embarrassment than we're going to get. Once the figures on Jay's theft come out, I'm afraid we're in for a siege of bad press."

"How much is it up to now?"

"I'm too embarrassed to tell you."

Talon hadn't been reluctant to talk when the total was fifty million dollars. My imagination had difficulty with an even higher number.

"Anyone see Jay?" I asked.

"Not even a hint," Talon said, shaking his head. "But we're working on it. We'll find him. And thank God for Parke! 'The Man Who Did The Right Thing.'" Talon stopped again and leaned toward me, speaking in a confidential tone. "Last night, I read his book. It's a damn good piece of writing. He really gave up a lot, having these letters rechecked."

"I can only guess," I replied, feeling a wave of guilt for taking away Parke Hollingshed's Pulitzer.

Then out of nowhere, Talon blurted, "I want to appoint him President of the Trust. We'll need someone like him to spearhead the rebuilding."

There are moments that defy description, lifting the burden of guilt. "Does Parke know about your plans?"

"Parke doesn't even know about Galbraith's report. Everybody on my staff is out looking for him."

Let's hope they have better luck finding Parke than they did Theodore Jay, I thought.

Rutherford Talon looked grim. His smile reappeared. "Thank you!" he said.

"For what?"

"For the advice you gave me: 'stay loose, hang tough, and think positive thoughts.' That it?"

I laughed, and hoped Parke Hollingshed would remember these words too when Talon offered him the Presidency of the Christian Historical Trust.

* * * * *

Just before closing, I heard another knock on my office door. It was Philip Norge.

"You accepting apologies?"

"You were just doing your job," I said, but I didn't mean it. I was still rankled.

"I came down on you pretty hard," Norge continued. "And all this time the letters were being analyzed in Washington."

"I don't mean to be rude," I said. "But I have another appointment."

I walked him to the door. It would take a long time for my feelings toward Norge to thaw.

* * * * *

At nine p.m., Parke Hollingshed appeared unannounced at my apartment. Hollingshed and I sat alone in the living room. Hope, anger, gratitude, and disbelief all seemed to register at the same time on Hollingshed's face. It was a trick equal to Talon's independently arching eyebrows.

"Talon catch up with you?"

"I don't know how you did it," Hollingshed said, "but I'm convinced you orchestrated this entire affair. Orchestrated it, wrote it, conducted it, and God knows what else."

I shrugged my shoulders. "What did you think of Galbraith's

report?"

"Think? I still don't know what to think! My whole world's turned upside down! I spent the last two years living like a monk, writing the Jefferson book. Now, I learn the letters were a hoax. They don't give Pulitzer Prizes for being taken in by hoaxes!

"Then, just when I'm scraping the bottom of my emotional barrel, Rutherford Talon offers me the Presidency of the Trust. Did you know he was going to?"

I shrugged my shoulders again. "The question is, did you accept?"

"Accept the job? Of course I accepted the job! It's beyond my wildest dreams."

Hollingshed gave his account of meeting Talon. At first, Hollingshed had been too stunned to deny he had sent the letters to Galbraith, then too morose to interrupt Talon's gushing praise, and by the time he had steeled himself and was ready to deny everything, Talon had offered him the Presidency.

"Only thing bothers me," Hollingshed said, "is getting the job under false pretenses. I didn't send Galbraith those letters."

"If you had suspected they were forgeries, you would have."

"A comforting thought, but I'll never know."

"Then regard the Presidency as a consolation prize for not winning the Pulitzer," I suggested. "You're not being offered something for nothing. The Christian Historical Trust is in trouble. They need a hero to rally the troops or they're going to fold. Like it or not, Parke, you're the only hero they've got."

By the time Hollingshed left, I saw a discernible shift in him from confusion to confidence. Parke Hollingshed would do just fine.

* * * * *

At this point I felt like a proud father. Jefferson might have felt pride about the Declaration of Independence, and God might have had similar emotions after creating the world. But unlike God, I didn't have an entire day to rest.

Fifteen minutes after Hollingshed's visit, the telephone rang.

"Somebody took a shot at me earlier this afternoon." It was Rutherford Talon sounding more shaken than he had when the trucks delivered *Jefferson, the Traitor.*

He had my full attention. "Where?"

"Outside the President's House, about five. The shot came from near the Capitol."

"Were you hurt?" I asked.

"No! Thank God! But the bullet did come within a foot of my head. I had just stepped back toward the house because I had forgotten my gloves."

"Where were your bodyguards?"

"Standing right next to me. They bundled me back inside before they left to look for the shooter. We called the police, naturally. They were no help, but it's a moot point. We didn't have to find him to know who the gunman was!"

"Where are you calling from?" I asked.

"Kingsmill. Timothy said it was the safest place to put me until they could get more security. He's probably right."

Ah, Kingsmill! I thought to myself.

"Join us. Parke Hollingshed's with me. We have plenty of room. You'll be safe. You don't want to be alone with Jay on the loose."

"Why should I worry? I'm not involved with the Trust."

"But Jay accused you of stealing the letters."

The thought of taking refuge in Kingsmill sent a shudder through my body. I thanked Talon for calling and assured him I'd be okay. Now all I had to do was assure myself.

* * * * *

I fell asleep reading *War and Peace.* When I was in college, a professor had told me a man should read Tolstoy's book three times in his life: in youth, middle age, and after. This was my third time through. I think I had subconsciously put off the final reading as a sort of hedge on immortality.

What woke me was the telephone.

"I did a very stupid thing," a gravelly voice told me.

"Galbraith?"

"A man who identified himself as a reporter for *The Washington Post* just called. He said he had a source who told him you sent the letters to me, but his editor insisted on confirmation before they ran the story. I don't know why, but I started to act coy, and said 'maybe.' Then the man hung up."

I was starting to comprehend what Galbraith was telling me. "And a real reporter would have stayed on the line."

"Precisely! I think I've put you in danger."

As soon as I was finished with Galbraith, I phoned Napoleon. "Now," I said. "I got a back needs watching." I heard shuffling sounds and the creaking of a bed in the background.

"You do pick the times," Napoleon said.

I told him about my calls from Talon and Galbraith.

"Stay put," he told me, "turn out the light, and don't open the door for anybody but me. Might be another half hour or so, but I'll be there."

Napoleon arrived just before midnight with a six-pack of Rolling Rock beer in long-neck bottles. When he removed his old leather flight jacket, I could see he was carrying a forty-five in a holster just under his left arm pit.

"You didn't see this," Napoleon said tapping the pistol. "Not legal for a convicted felon to carry a weapon, but I thought tonight might be worth the risk."

Napoleon went around the house turning on lights and lowering shades. "This way if Jay shows up, he won't know what room we in."

Napoleon and I spent most of the night sitting at the oak table in my kitchen quietly sipping beer and listening to the house creak.

About a half hour went by before Napoleon asked, "You and Kate having problems?"

I gave my best impression of a deer caught in head lights.

"Don't mean to pry. Just wanted you to know I'm sorry if it's true."

"What did Kate tell you?" I asked, straining for details.

"She didn't go into the blow by blows, but I figured her life with you was behind her proposal."

"Napoleon, what are you talking about?"

"Kate, she asked me to think of a price Chili and I would be willing to pay for her share of Chez Bayou."

I felt an empty panic inside and watched as the room began to spin.

"You okay?" I heard Napoleon say from far away.

"Yeah," I heard myself respond. I was too busy concentrating on passing out to say anything more.

"Nothing's been decided," Napoleon continued, trying to soften the blow. "Near as I can tell, she just testing the waters. Asking the hypotheticals."

I looked at Napoleon. His face was creased with concern.

"You didn't know, did you?" he asked.

"We were having problems," I said, "but I didn't know she was making plans to leave."

We both took another swig of beer. I wiped the perspiration off my forehead with a paper napkin.

"Sometimes it happens with a woman like Kate," Napoleon said. "Nobody's fault. Fact is, things going well between the two of you, you getting close to Kate probably was the trigger."

"I'm not following."

"Kate's survived in her life by building a cocoon 'round herself. You penetrated the cocoon and now she's scared."

"Scared of what?"

"Scared she's going to lose herself. Scared she's going to end up just being a part of you. Scared she going to miss something in life."

"Ridiculous."

"*Ridiculous* to you, maybe, but *real* to Kate." Napoleon went to the refrigerator and opened another bottle of beer. "You and me, Brad, we know who we are. Kate? Behind the outer confidence, I'm not sure she do. Only way she feel safe is to put the cocoon around herself again." Napoleon pointed at his beer. "Want one?"

I shook my head.

"You think back, you'll remember things she said. Guarantee you, you were warned!"

I remembered my fortune-telling dream.

"You just didn't pay attention." Napoleon took a gulp from the long neck bottle. "See, I know. I was hurt by a woman just like Kate, but it wouldn't happen now."

"What changed?"

"I don't rush into nothing; take my time getting involved. Look for signs, and if I see them, I'm gone. Kick 'em to the curb!"

I looked hard at Napoleon and laughed. "Like Goldilocks?"

"Goldilocks is recreational sex! I'm recreational sex for her, too. In fact, I'm a whole playground, the way she tell it. We could see a glint in each other's eyes, so we talked about it just after the party."

I audibly sighed. "I don't know, Napoleon."

"Well, I do! Don't let this get you down. Relationship breaking up wasn't your fault. It was going to happen sooner or later. Be glad it didn't last any longer. Just don't let it happen again. Take a long while for a man and woman to create a web of trust, 'specially now we get older. I were you, I'd be asking myself what I wanted a relationship for and why I was attracted to a women like Kate in the first place. Most men would have run the other way."

* * * * *

By morning no one had made an attempt to kill me. Spending what was left of the evening thinking about Kate, I half wished someone had. In the morning Napoleon called Chili. "This a two-man back watchin' project now!" he told me.

"It isn't necessary."

"I the back-watcher!" Napoleon said. "I decide!"

Napoleon and Chili alternated shadowing my every move. It was unnerving. I probably wouldn't have done much work in any event, preoccupied as I was with Kate, but the bathroom was the only place where I could be alone. In the evening, Napoleon went to work at Chez Bayou. Chili made dinner for Kate and me at my apartment. It was the first Kate and I had seen each other in three days. Dinner was fine. Kate wore a happy face. I didn't. I kept wondering if Napoleon had told Kate about our conversation the night before. I was looking for clues in everything Kate said and did. My paranoia was in overdrive. I was angry and upset Kate hadn't talked to me about leaving. I thought back to Abbe not discussing a divorce with Peter. Was I a frightening man? After a while, my sullen mood began to affect Kate. During dinner, she didn't say a word. We cleared the table and Chili turned on the television. The noise from sit-com babble was the final straw.

"Damn it!" I screamed at no one in particular.

Kate looked up at me as if I were some sort of slimy creature crawling out from underneath her bed.

"I'm going!" I said.

"Where?" Kate asked coolly. "The bookshop?"

I didn't answer.

"I go with you," Chili said.

"No! Stay with Kate."

"Napoleon said..."

"I don't care what Napoleon said!"

"But Napoleon won't like this."

Kate stood. "I guess it really doesn't matter what you do."

I grabbed my jacket with the car keys in the pocket and left them both, slamming the door behind me.

Chapter Twenty-six

೭✿⋅ಌ

Once I was in my own car driving to the bookshop, I was fine. Fine and ashamed. I knew better than to allow anger to build up inside me. I would have talked to Kate except Chili had been there. What I should have done—should have done but didn't—was to have Chili wait outside while we had our conversation. I just didn't think about it at the time. Once I got to the office, I told myself, I would call Kate and set up a time for us to have our face-to-face. I might be losing Kate, but at least I could tell her how I felt and see, one last time, if there was a way to keep the relationship afloat. I was afraid it was too late but I still wanted to make the effort.

I parked my car in the free lot behind the shop. The lot was almost empty. It was night and the shops were closed. Only Rustermann's was open and even it was gearing down. Williamsburg was fast becoming a retirement community and people tended to eat early.

Opening the bookshop door, I felt a hard, sharp object against the small of my back.

"Not funny, Napoleon," I said without turning around.

Then I heard the cultured but insistent voice of Theodore Jay, "You've got an alarm system to turn off," he said.

All my life I had trained myself not to panic. It was a good thing because I needed all the reserve I could find. I went over to the wall behind the counter and tapped in my personal pass code. It turned off the alarm system. I flipped on the overhead lights and turned to face him.

Jay had what could have been a hand gun underneath the raincoat draped over his arm. He held his arm parallel to the ground like an old-fashioned waiter carrying a white towel, and positioned himself with his back toward the windows.

"You have a gun?" I asked.

Jay lifted the raincoat with his left hand enough for me to see. A crooked, bent smile washed over his face.

"What the hell are you doing with a gun?" It wasn't a phrase from the *Hostage Negotiator's Handbook*, but it was on my mind, so I asked it. Despite all the warnings and precautions, I'd actually never expected to see Jay again, except in a courtroom.

"Isn't it obvious? I'm going to shoot you."

Jay spoke evenly, with a cool, imperious demeanor. It was only when I looked into his eyes I saw the unsettled and dangerous rage within. It was like looking directly into the mouth of a volcano.

The full danger of the situation began to penetrate. I had been given back-up, but in my anger, I had left it far behind. I was alone. In the espionage business, this was a rookie mistake—a potentially fatal rookie mistake.

"I could kill you here," Jay said. "But I prefer we take a walk."

My mind raced. The world around me seemed to be in slow motion. From the corner of my eye, I saw Gordon sitting on the counter watching the scene quietly, ever hopeful, probably wondering which of us would stop to feed him. I glanced at Bruce's shipping room wondering where the aluminum baseball bat was.

"Enough time," Jay said as if he were reading my mind. "Turn out the light and put the alarm system back on."

My eyes hadn't spotted a suitable weapon. I toyed with the idea of throwing Gordon at Jay, but then what? I could refuse to go, of course, but I was certain if I did, Jay would kill me where I stood. Zealots and crazed people! So I obediently turned off the lights. The room was still well-lit from the glow of Rustermann's Restaurant across the walkway.

"The alarm system," Jay reminded me.

I tapped in the numbers one-seven-six-seven—one s.o.s. It was a code I had worked out with the security company years before in case of a robbery. I had never used the code and I doubted they still remembered.

Jay waved his arm with the raincoat, motioning me toward the door. As I passed Gordon, I could see a look of dismay on his face, wondering why there was no food. There's a lot to be said for guard dogs.

I spent as much time as I could locking up. I felt Jay's impatience. My only plan was to keep Jay from shooting me for as long as possible. I would wait for an opportunity to either escape or take the gun away. I wondered if Jews stepping into Nazi gas chambers had similar plans going through their heads.

For me, help might still be on the way. The security company, the police, Napoleon. I should never have gone to the shop alone.

Jay waved his draped arm again, directing me through the archway, away from Duke of Gloucester Street.

"Where to?"

"You'll see."

A secondary plan: keep Jay talking, distract him, gain an advantage. Even when I thought it, I knew it wasn't much of a plan, but I was desperate.

"Why are you doing this?" I asked Jay. "You have more money than you could spend in a lifetime."

"Money isn't everything," Jay responded.

"What else do you want?"

"Revenge!"

"Revenge for what?"

"For exposing the Jefferson letters as forgeries. For ruining my life."

"Your life was ruined when you stole fifty million dollars from the Trust."

"Eighty million dollars," Jay corrected me smugly.

I turned around. Jay was standing two long steps behind me. He was too far away for me to lunge at him and too near to for me to run. We were in the middle of the parking lot. I was trying my best to look unruffled, so I put my hands in my trouser pockets. There I found an accumulation of loose change.

"Why do you want to kill me?" I rephrased my only question.

Jay smiled wickedly, "Because it's payback time. Sometimes it's getting even *and* living well. Now, keep walking!"

As I turned, I brought out a clump of change in my clenched fist. I thought of throwing the twenty or so coins at Jay, but realized he could easily put a round through my chest before the money even hit him. Instead I dropped two quarters on the ground. Jay didn't seem to notice.

We walked through the small parking lot behind the Goodwin Building, where, like Hansel with his bread crumbs, I dropped another coin. There was only a very slim chance anyone would see the trail I was leaving, but like my plan with the Jefferson letters, it was all I could think of at the time.

When we got to Prince George Street, Jay said, "Turn right."

I dropped another coin.

"What do you think you're doing?" Jay hissed. "Leaving a trail?"

I was too afraid to answer.

"Truly pathetic! Go ahead, if it makes you feel better. It's dark. No one could follow your silly little trail even if they guessed what it might be."

Jay was right, but it didn't stop me. We crossed Henry Street. Jay had us both walk down the middle of Prince George. There was no traffic and nothing to grab or throw at Jay here. Behind me,

I thought I heard the siren of a police car, probably rushing to my aid. A lot of good, I thought. We walked down the dimly lit street.

As we approached Nassau Street, Jay barked a single syllable, "Left!" So much for keeping him talking and distracted. I continued dropping my coins, wondering how far we had to go and hoping I wouldn't run out of loose change before we got there.

"Who made the Jefferson letters for you? Peter Mosely?" I asked.

The street was considerably darker now. "It was a collaborative effort," Jay replied. "I did the scholarship, which I must say was flawless, and Peter produced the physical letters."

"It must have taken a long time."

Jay didn't answer immediately. I turned around. Jay was a safe distance behind me. "Just keep walking," he said.

I did. A few steps later I asked, "How long have you been working on this project?"

"I know what you're trying to do. You're trying to distract me," Jay said, "but it won't work!"

"At this point," I asked, "what's the harm? Don't you want someone to know how smart you've been?"

He considered this. "Yes," he finally said. "I have nothing to lose. And yes, it did take a long time to prepare the letters. I began serious work over four years ago, long before Rutherford Talon was elected to the board. Tweaking him was the unexpected bonus!"

"Where did you find the writing paper?" I asked.

"Very astute of you," Jay answered. "The paper, of course, was the source of my inspiration. I bought it from a bookseller in the small town of Buren in the Netherlands. It was a very rare find, two thousand sheets of a fine eighteenth century writing paper. French, you know. Something Thomas Jefferson could have bought in Paris and brought back with him to the United States. Without the paper, there would have been no Jefferson letters.

"Anyone could duplicate eighteenth century iron gaul ink. No problem. The paper was the key."

"Who physically wrote the letters?"

"Oh, Peter," Jay said. "He was an art major in college and quite the calligrapher. I think he outdid himself. Don't you?"

We were almost to Scotland Street when Jay stopped his narrative and ordered me to turn right, pointing to a narrow dirt footpath. It was an unexpected route so I dropped three coins here. I was familiar with this little-used dirt walkway. It went past the Governor's Palace gardens. There was a five-foot-high brick wall to the left.

"Don't even think of trying to leap over it," Jay said. "If you do, I might shoot you for fun and watch you bleed to death here."

"Thanks!" I replied.

"My pleasure, I'm sure," Jay cooed.

The path was lit by a sparse line of tallow street lamps. The wall to the left was seductively low. Twenty years earlier, before countless dinners at Rustermann's and Chez Bayou, I could have scaled it and escaped by running along the far side. Now, like the clever concentration camp inmate I had imagined, I kept walking along the path, waiting, avoiding being shot like an East Berliner of another time.

"How did Peter learn to age the ink?" I asked. The purpose of my questions now had subtly changed. I was no longer trying to distract Jay. Now, I was talking to keep myself from panic. I could viscerally feel Jay behind me like an animal who sensed fear in his prey.

"He experimented first by himself," Jay answered. "Then he went to Utah to talk to a prisoner he had heard about—someone who knew the technique."

"How did Peter find him?"

"Peter Mosely knew many strange people."

"Did Peter's contact go to prison for forgery?" I asked.

"Murder actually! But the man was able to explain some of his forgery techniques to Peter and put him on the right track."

"But why bother creating the letters in the first place?" I asked.

"The simple answer to your complex question is I did my doctoral thesis on Jefferson," Jay explained. "God, how I grew to hate T.J.!"

"And he was the one person Rutherford Talon admired."

"Worshipped!" Jay said. "So in one act, I had the opportunity to ruin Jefferson's reputation and destroy Talon's idol. The bonus was leaving him in charge of a financially depleted Christian Historical Trust, an organization to be forever linked with the discovery of Jefferson's infamous act. And everything might have worked if it hadn't been for you."

"I was only one of many. Peter Mosely tried to stop you first, didn't he?" I guessed.

"Ah, Peter. And Peter Mosley died for his efforts. You see, he got greedy. Peter made a second set of Jefferson letters which he tried to sell to a customer in New York."

"Anthony Calvado."

"Very good, Brad," Jay said. "Yes! Anthony Calvado! Unfortunately for Peter, Mr. Calvado called me because he heard a rumor we owned the letters."

"What did you tell him?"

"We owned the letters and Peter had never been given authority to sell them. Now it was a matter of whom he trusted most, me or Peter Mosley. Given the choice, it was easy for Mr. Calvado to believe what I had told him and to back away from any deal with Peter. Peter inspired paranoia in everyone who dealt with him. All I did was to grease the pole."

"And kill him!"

"In my position, wouldn't you?"

We were on the far side of the path now, in front of the Governor's Palace. I spun around to face Jay. My movement was too abrupt. I immediately knew I had made a mistake. By the street light, I could see the hammer of Jay's revolver inching backward. I froze, not risking another overt movement.

Fractions of seconds felt like minutes. I didn't know if Jay was going to continue to squeeze the trigger or not. I don't think he knew himself, or if he were skillful enough with a handgun to stop it from happening. My throat constricted; my breathing stopped; sweat filled my pores.

Then I saw the hammer slowly return to where it had been. We had both teetered on the edge between control and madness.

I took a deep breath before I asked my next question. "Why did you kill Abbe?"

"I didn't," Jay answered. "Peter killed his wife. He came back to the house and found her stealing more Jefferson letters. Abbe ran up to her bedroom and Peter followed. Peter told me he hit her over the head with a large German Bible less than fifteen minutes before I had arrived at the house."

"But you were the one who killed Peter and started the fire," I prompted.

"Yes! With a can of gasoline Peter kept for his lawn mower," Jay explained. "Peter's letters were the only evidence our's were forgeries. So, I had to burn his house because I didn't know if Peter had any more letters lying around. And I was forced to kill Peter, because if he had lived, he would have blackmailed me. It was all inevitable."

"You were doomed from the start, Jay. Even if Galbraith hadn't gotten his hands on your letters, scholars still would have disputed your claim."

"How? I had written appraisals from three experts stating the letters were authentic. If scholars got too close, the letters would tragically have been destroyed in an accidental fire, leaving only the photocopies. Nobody could prove a case of forgery from a photocopy. Thomas Jefferson's reputation would have remained tarnished."

Another question tweaked my curiosity. "How much did you pay Peter for his part in the scheme?" I asked.

"A half million dollars! I also had to pay Peter a salary for a year out of my own pocket so he could concentrate on the project."

Perhaps Jay wanted me to feel sorry for him. Instead I dropped another quarter.

A wind blew through the trees. Clouds drifted past uncovering a three-quarter moon.

"But enough," Jay said, raising his gun menacingly in front of him. "Walk!"

"Where?"

"Up Nicholson Street to my house."

"The President's house? Talon is there."

"Talon and his bodyguards are at Kingsmill this evening. Parke Hollingshed is with them along with the police."

I didn't want to know, but I had to. "Why are we going there?" I asked.

"Because when Talon returns, I want him to find your body in the basement next to the sixty thousand copies of Parke Hollingshed's magnum opus, *Jefferson, The Traitor*. I've dreamed about the tableau. Now walk or I'll kill you here. It's still your choice."

We walked down Spotswood Street along the Palace Green and made a left turn at Nicholson. As we did, I dropped the last of my pocket change. I knew Jay was right. The chance of someone following my trail was about as good as winning the Virginia State Lottery.

Neither of us talked. We passed the Peyton Randolph House. The Courthouse Green was to my right. I could see no one on the streets. Quietly we passed the Cabinetmaker's House and the Carpenter's Yard. The wind was picking up ominously. No doubt, there was a winter cold front coming from the west, a cold front, the results of which, I would most likely never see.

We were almost to the Public Gaol when I looked off to the right and saw Jefferson standing next to a large oak. He seemed to be talking to someone.

"Keep walking," Jay said behind me.

Then I saw Jefferson make a wild, windmill gesture with his arms, and for the first time I was aware of the large horned owl rising from a low branch next to where Jefferson was standing. He flew directly at us, no more than six feet off the ground, like a bomber pilot avoiding radar, propelled by the slow, powerful strokes of his wings.

At the last moment, Jay saw the owl too. I heard him cry, "Wha...," but it was too late. The owl had flown directly at Jay's face and had sunk his talons into Jay's cheeks. Jay screamed into the night.

It was my chance. I didn't hesitate. I ran down Nicholson and made an abrupt right toward the bridge leading to the Capitol. I could hear Jay's screams and curses behind me. I was on the bridge, half way across it, when I felt a rush of air go through my body. I became aware I wasn't walking any more. I was flat on the ground, scrambling to get up on my hands and knees.

I looked to the far side of the bridge. I could see a searing white light and smooth chrome-yellow ground. Jefferson was standing there along with my dead wife, Phyllis, and our two sons. They were shouting at me, urging me on as if I were a marathon runner struggling through the last few yards, giving my all to reach the finish line. I thought I saw Abbe standing behind Phyllis.

From the other end of the bridge, I heard noises and scuffling. I wasn't coordinated enough to turn around. My body wouldn't respond anymore, and besides, the light in front of me had become increasingly mesmerizing. All the people in the light began to chant, "Brad! Brad!" Phyllis was calling to me. I could see everyone in the light so clearly. I remember thinking the light end of the bridge would be such a nice, peaceful place to be. I became aware of trying to scream. "No!" I seemed to have said the word more within my head than with my mouth, as if something deep inside was tethering me to life. "No!" The word echoed inside me before the onset of the excruciating pain and the resulting blackness.

Chapter Twenty-seven

I drifted between the darkness and the light and back again. If time existed, it had no meaning. When I was in the light, I had long conversations with Phyllis and my boys. I can't remember what we said, but I do recall the peace and tranquility I felt during those talks. The warmth and love from our past had remained. Our problems with each other had been anesthetized.

I was so absorbed when I was engaged in the light I didn't think of my own state of being. In between the periods of light was the darkness, so complete and enveloping I became one with the void itself.

The cycle of darkness and light—my yin and yang—was repeated again and again, until I finally came into a grey place and moaned from a searing pain in my stomach.

"Glad you decided to join the land of the living," a voice said. It was Napoleon's.

"I'm alive," I answered.

"'Course you alive. This ain't heaven and I ain't no angel!"

"Where am I?" I could hear the dry, crackled timbre of my own weak voice.

"Williamsburg Hospital. I carried you in here myself, ten days ago."

Ten days! I slipped back into unconsciousness, hoping to return to the light, but I never made it back. When I woke next, Kate was holding my hand. She leaned down and kissed my forehead. Warm tears fell to my cheeks.

"I thought you had gone," was all she said. She squeezed my hand and cried.

The next day was better. The nurses raised my bed to a forty-five degree angle and hand-spooned bouillon and jello into my mouth. Intensive Care rationed my visitors to five minute intervals. Eventually, I was able to piece together the story of what had happened.

Napoleon and Chili had arrived at Parker's Rare Books within five minutes of my leaving it. They met the police, who were called there by the alarm company. They *had* remembered my emergency code after all. Napoleon explained about Jay and the attempted shooting of Talon. The police said they would search the area on the far side of the Duke of Gloucester, and Napoleon and Chili went in the other direction. Napoleon had borrowed a flashlight from one of the policemen.

In the dark and empty parking lot, Napoleon had seen a coin on the ground and found a second one on Prince George Street. "I remembered our talk way back when, about leaving a trail of bread crumbs, and I had said `This is America, you got to leave a trail of money!' I figured only a crazy white man would actually attempt such a dumb thing, but then I said to myself, `Hell, Brad *is* a crazy white man.'"

So Napoleon turned on the flashlight and he and Chili started to follow the coins. Chili was the one who saw the quarters I dropped at the entrance to the path along the Palace Gardens. Napoleon spotted the last coin at the corner of Nicholson Street. According to him, they were a hundred yards behind us when they heard the shot. "We saw Jay running toward the President's House. Chili ran after him. I went looking for you."

Apparently, I had been difficult to find in the dark, but Napoleon finally managed. My pulse was weak and erratic. The bullet had pierced a main artery. Napoleon saw an incredible pool of blood under and around me and was frightened. He gathered me up in his arms and carried me up to the Duke of Gloucester Street by the Capitol. There, he was met by a security officer.

"The jerk stood by his car, telling me about how CW policy wouldn't allow him to take an injured person to the hospital. I listened respectful and all. You were lying across the trunk of the car. Finally, I said 'what the hell' and threw a hard right, kind of knocked the man out."

"Kind of?"

"He was on his knees, but his only thought was of flying with the birdies. Then, I borrowed the security car and bundled you into the back seat. If I waited a few minutes, we wouldn't be here having this conversation." Napoleon paused and added. "'Cept maybe if you was a ghost."

* * * * *

Late on my second day of consciousness, Alida came with a container of chicken soup in a plain brown paper bag. I told her about my memory of meeting dead people in the light at the end of the bridge. I told her of talking with Abbe there.

"What did she say?" Alida asked.

"Can't remember," I told her. "But we both felt an incredible feeling of peace."

Alida's smile showed her pleasure. "I'm glad," she told me. "It's good to think Abbe's finally at rest."

* * * * *

Norge came to see me in the evening. He told me they had had no luck finding Jay and posted a guard by the door of my hospital room. Before he left Norge paused as if he were about to say something, stopped himself, and went out the door, the words unsaid. I drifted back to sleep.

* * * * *

Rutherford Talon came for a visit the next morning carrying a large plastic-wrapped fruit basket.

"Can the Christian Historical Trust afford this?" I asked.

"No, but I can."

There was still no news of Jay. Except for his visit to the hospital, Talon stayed at Kingsmill with Hollingshed. They talked of the future. By then his auditors had managed to trace ten million dollars to the Bahamas. "It's frozen while our lawyers start the process of recovering it. At least it's a start!"

"And the books!" Talon finally said. *The New York Times* had picked up on the story of Jay's embezzlement and *Jefferson the Traitor*. They favorably reviewed it in their Sunday book section as a non-fiction novel. Then orders started coming from Amazon.com and Barnes and Noble. "The response has been overwhelming. We might have to go into a second printing."

* * * * *

Even Max Durgan came, with a large box of Godiva chocolates, wearing his outlandish three-piece hounds-tooth suit. We exchanged the pleasant remarks strangers do under such circumstances. All the while I waited for him to tell me Thomas Jefferson was a hologram-hoax, but Durgan never did. I still hadn't given up hope that Durgan could give me a logical explanation for everything.

* * * * *

Parke Hollingshed arrived the next day full of news about his first days as President of the Christian Historical Trust. I smiled and let him blather. I was right about him: he was going to be all right.

* * * * *

Later Galbraith phoned, apologizing again in his raspy voice about the trouble he had caused. Eventually, he returned the Jefferson letter, the one Abbe had brought to the shop. Now it's framed in my office as a memento.

* * * * *

While I was in the hospital, Bruce gave me regular reports on what had been happening with Parker Rare Books. He was doing a remarkable job taking up the slack. He even bought well, which surprised me. When I recovered, I'd have to reassess our relationship.

One day he showed up at the hospital with Gordon in a traveling cat box. Gordon seemed please to see me, but the nurses were not amused.

*****

I had expected to have another visit by Thomas Jefferson, but he didn't come. It depressed me to think I had seen the last of him. This surprised me.

"Kind of grows on you," Napoleon said, after I mentioned my disappointment.

"You'd think he would have come to thank us or just say goodbye."

"Yeah," Napoleon mused. "I always thought he was a peckerhead, but I would have expected him to at least say goodbye."

We sat in silence.

"You ever think, though," Napoleon said. "You ever think maybe he settled his debt sending the owl after Jay?"

"You mean maybe Jefferson isn't a ghost any more?"

"Or if he is, maybe we can't see him."

In the months following, part of me anticipated looking up and seeing Jefferson, but I never did. I also took walks around Williamsburg looking for the owl. All in vain.

*****

Recovering in the hospital gave me time to think about Kate. She visited every day, but I could sense it was over between us. Two weeks into my recovery, Napoleon told me their offer for Kate's stock had been accepted.

Two days later Kate told me she was leaving. She said we just wanted different things out of life, and we did. I wanted to be involved in a warm and caring relationship, Kate didn't. I didn't express it to her in those words, but from my point of view, it's an apt epitaph for what we had together. You can't keep a relationship going if one person stops wanting it. After that there's nothing left to do but let go.

For the most part, I didn't feel anger anymore, and I didn't try to talk Kate out of her decision. I had to concentrate on moving on. It was going to take me longer than Kate. My psyche was as bruised and tender as my body. I lay in the hospital thinking about what had attracted me to Kate in the first place. Maybe I had been afraid of a relationship, too. I wouldn't have thought so and I couldn't tell you how I expressed this, but we're all attracted to people with the same general traits we have. I had a lot to ponder—especially since I didn't want to repeat this scenario.

* * * * *

Napoleon picked up Kate at the hospital at seven o'clock the night before I was to be released. There still had been no sightings of Jay, and Norge had finally pulled his twenty-four hour watch from outside my room.

"We going out to try the food at Rustermann's tonight," Napoleon said.

"You've been eating out a lot lately."

"Pretty much since you were shot," Napoleon said.

"Your holiday spectaculars not appealing?"

Kate and Napoleon exchanged glances. Neither of them spoke for a long while.

"You see," Kate began. "Nobody's seen Theodore Jay."

"Chili ran after him," Napoleon continued. "Then this Jay, he disappeared, just like the guard at Sewell, George Granton."

"Given Chili's past, both of us are reluctant to eat at Chez Bayou," Kate concluded. "Especially the meat dishes!"

"Did you ask Chili about this?"

"Hell no," Napoleon answered. "Don't seem to be none of my business."

"I probably wouldn't believe anything he said, anyway," Kate added.

"No matter what really happened, Chili always going to be Chili. I'm just happy we have the same pot-boy for two months running," said Napoleon.

Whatever the truth about Chili, I didn't really care either. My goals centered around getting out of the hospital and once again being with Gordon. They weren't lofty aspirations, but you have to start somewhere.